For my sister.
Because complacency is the most dangerous place to be.

INTRODUCTION

I began writing this story on an old yellow legal pad while on vacation with my family in the Outer Banks. The ending came to me first. It played in a loop over-and-over again in my head enough for me to know that I had to write it down. I didn't know how the story would unfold. I just knew how it had to end.

At the time, I figured my love of writing would be enough to carry me through to the finish. Not so much. Writing a book is a lot like trying to pick up paper clips on a waxed wooden floor with mittens. Is it possible? Sure. Is it frustrating? Hell yes!

I got plenty of bumps and bruises along the way. And I mean that both figuratively and literally. There's just something about writer's block that makes you want to flip tables. In the beginning, especially, I felt like I was losing direction.

During one of those particularly frustrating periods of writers' block, I was checking my e-mail when I saw an alumni newsletter from my high school alma mater. In it, they highlighted their most recent Super Dance (a twelve-hour dance-a-thon that raises money and awareness for Cystic Fibrosis). I soon found myself deep in the interweb, reading blog posts and watching videos of people living with the disease. Their blunt honesty, positive disposition, and passion to find a cure was inspiring. They gave me direction.

I want to make it very clear: this story does not represent those affected by Cystic Fibrosis as a whole. Cystic Fibrosis is an unrelenting and ever-changing genetic disease. It affects every individual differently; some can run marathons, others are bedridden. Currently, there's no cure but life expectancy continues to rise and new developments in medication and treatment are helping us get closer to finding one.

While this story's foundation is based on real people and real situations, it's still fiction. It doesn't come close to describing the reality of living with Cystic Fibrosis. But I hope that it will open your eyes to this disease—a disease that's often hidden behind a brave façade.

We all can spread awareness and I encourage you to start the conversation. However, if you happen to have the time or money, please consider contributing to the Cystic Fibrosis Foundation. In fact, just purchasing this book has made a difference in the fight against Cystic Fibrosis. It's my promise to you that 50% of this book's proceeds will go to the Cystic Fibrosis Foundation.

With that said, I'm proud to present to you *View from the Edge*. Thank you for taking a chance on this book. I hope you enjoy reading it as much as I've enjoyed finally finishing it.

I want to stand as close to the edge as I can without going over. Out on the edge you see all the kinds of things you can't see from the center.
-Kurt Vonnegut

PROLOGUE
The Espresso Machine

The rich smell of ground coffee and freshly cooked bacon was beginning to make Ben feel nauseous as he waited for Molly to continue. The couple sat across from one another at a stunted wooden table in a small café downtown. The walls echoed with muffled chatter and clinking cups. But all Ben could hear was the deafening silence that filled the space between them.

"I think we should go on a break," Molly finally said.

Ben nodded but wouldn't look at her. Instead, he focused his brooding stare on her plain egg white omelet.

"Say something," she pleaded.

"I know some great movers," he mumbled.

"Ben…"

"What do you want me to say?" He shrugged.

"Well, for starters, maybe you could fight for us for once?"

"What's that supposed to mean?"

"I mean it's no secret that we've been in a rut."

"So, you're bored and thought a fight would make things more interesting?"

"No, I want you to just… stop going through the motions!" she sputtered before leaning back in her chair and sighing.

"Going through the motions?" Ben spat, his voice growing louder.

Neighboring coffee drinkers tilted their heads, interested in what the cause for yelling could be on this cool Saturday morning. Ben ignored them.

"So, asking you to move in with me was going through the motions?"

Molly rolled her eyes. "Ben, please. You're making a scene."

"I'm what?"

Their neighbors shifted uncomfortably in their seats. One sharp dressed man gulped down the rest of his latte and hurried out the clear shop doors.

Now Ben was furious. Not only had Molly chosen to have a very personal conversation with him in public but she was acting as if his reaction was irrational.

"Oh, I'm sorry," Ben said holding his hands up in defense, "should I not be making a scene? Excuse me..." Leaning to the left Ben caught the attention of an elderly couple sipping chai tea and sharing a blueberry scone. "Would you make a scene if your girlfriend of six months decided to break up with you in public for absolutely no reason?"

His victims looked at each other, desperately hoping the other would come up with an appropriate response. Luckily, Ben gave up on them and shifted his weight to his right side.

"Ben!"

"How about you?" he continued, directing his question to a woman wearing a Georgetown sweatshirt and typing on a laptop.

"Should I be okay with my girlfriend of six months breaking up with me in public for absolutely no reason?"

Without even glancing up from her laptop the woman replied with a simple, "Nope."

Satisfied, Ben sat back in his chair. "You're so immature."

"So, that's why you're breaking up with me?"

"I said we should go on a break."

"What's the difference?"

Molly paused for a moment and looked down at her coffee. "It's Olivia. I'm uncomfortable with your relationship."

"Not this again." Ben pinched the bridge of this nose.

"I thought I could do it, but I can't. I'm sick of coming second in your life."

"You're not second," he said with a sigh. But as soon as the words left his lips, he knew it was a lie and guilt began building in his gut.

"You see her almost every day. You talk to her all the time—"

"Olivia's one of my best friends. What do you want me to do?"

"Answer one question for me," she said. "You're in love with her, aren't you?"

It sounded more like an accusation than a question but Ben wasn't about to point that out. Instead, his tension melted and he suddenly felt vulnerable.

"What?" he said weakly, his mind going blank.

"Just answer the question, Ben."

"I… look, I will always care about Olivia," he began.

"You'll never be happy with me, will you?" Molly whispered as a single tear rolled down her cheek.

Their audience didn't bother hiding their eavesdropping now. Nearby customers froze and silence filled the air as everyone waited to see what would happen next.

"Molly, don't… let's talk about this."

"I'm not the one you're in love with and I never will be." She wiped her eyes as she gathered her purse and stood.

"Wait."

She stopped and looked down at him, her eyebrows raised.

"I'd like to keep the espresso machine." The words spilled out before he could stop them.

Molly's mouth fell open in shock. "Go to Hell," she said venomously before storming through the clear shop doors and out of sight.

✳ ✳ ✳

"And that's when she started crying," Ben said as he looked down at the garlic he was chopping. It now resembled a sticky paste after recounting the breakup to his fellow sous chef, Pete. The two stood side-by-side in the middle of a hectic restaurant kitchen, prepping food for the night ahead.

"Wow man, that sucks," Pete said as he stirred a bubbling béchamel sauce. "You're going to have to find a new brunch place. It's tainted now."

"I'm glad you see what's important here," Ben replied sarcastically.

"What's important is that it ended. You two never had any… sparks."

"Before she left, I told her I wanted to keep the espresso machine."

Pete spun around to face him. "You're joking."

Ben shrugged sheepishly. "It just came out."

"First, you told her you loved Olivia. Then you said: I'd like to keep the espresso machine?"

"I never said I loved Olivia."

"I hate to tell you this, but you've got a voodoo doll with your name on it."

Vexed, Ben flung the mushy garlic aside and picked up the specials menu. "Why is the avocado gazpacho still on here?" he mumbled.

For a moment, he thought about suggesting they serve a creamy wild rice and mushroom soup. But Ben shook his head and tossed the menu aside. Chef Jetter never liked his ideas anyway.

He'd always wanted to open his own restaurant and now seemed as good a time as any. His grandfather left him some money when he passed away last year. It wasn't much but it might be enough to help him break free of this place.

"Look on the bright side: I've got my wing-man back!" Pete said, interrupting his thoughts. He gave him a swift slap on the shoulder. "You know what you need?"

"A cliff to jump off of?"

"A night out. You can get wasted and take home—"

"No thanks."

"Just one little one-night-stand?"

"I'm not using someone to get over Molly," Ben insisted. "Plus, maybe we just need a little time apart," he added but then immediately winced.

"Ben, two words: *espresso machine*." He moved his hand from left to right as if the words were spelled out in the air in front of him. "It's over and I'm telling you: one-night-stand, one-night-stand, one-night-stand."

Ben shook his head. Pete wasn't exactly the person who should be giving out relationship advice. His idea of a romantic night was ordering Chinese and watching Saturday Night Live. But he had to admit, Pete was right... at least the part about it being over with Molly.

"Or, you know, you can just cut to the chase and have your rebound be Olivia."

"Don't go there."

Pete raised his palms up in innocence. "I'm just trying to point you in the direction of your soul mate. Have you told her yet by the way?"

"No, not yet." Ben wiped his hands on a clean towel and sighed.

I'm not the one you're in love with. Molly's words echoed in his head. He didn't want to admit it, but the first person he thought of when Molly walked out was Olivia and that terrified him.

CHAPTER ONE
Tick Tock

The sun was directly overhead by the time Olivia pulled into the Capital Medical Center parking lot. With her phone pressed to her ear, she listened to her voice messages and jogged to the entrance. She was late. Again.

> *Hey, honey. You're probably already at your appointment but I just wanted to call and remind you that you promised dinner tomorrow night...*

Olivia cursed and pocketed her phone. Her father knew her too well. She had forgotten but it was too late to cancel now.

The hospital's automatic doors opened and she wove her way through the activity in the atrium. Sunlight streamed through the glass ceiling, patrons and personnel gave her a warm "hello" or smile as she passed, and the scent of lemons permeated the air.

Olivia had been part of the Cystic Fibrosis Program since she was diagnosed as a baby. The doctors and nurses were like a second family and, with only about 100 patients in the hospital's entire Cystic Fibrosis program, walking through the hospital doors felt a lot like coming home. But, as welcoming as this place was, it didn't change the reason why she had to drag herself in every other month.

She caught the elevator door just before it closed and was relieved to find it empty. As she stepped into the cabin, she could no longer ignore the tightness in her chest and broke out in a fit of phlegmy coughs. Pulling out her inhaler, she punched the level three button and began taking deep grateful breaths. The shiny chrome doors closed with a squeak and she suddenly came face-to-face with her reflection.

"Yikes," she said and dropped her inhaler back into her bag. She gazed back at the two icy blue eyes in front of her and tried to see the beauty her mother always talked about. But all she could see was paper-pale skin, sunken eyes, and wispy blonde hair.

Olivia shook her head and looked away. There was absolutely nothing beautiful about Cystic Fibrosis. Her lungs were drowning in thick, sticky mucus, she was grumpy from constant exhaustion, and her frail, thin figure left little to desire.

She tapped her foot impatiently as the elevator crept past level two. Every time she came here she felt like she had to prepare herself for bad news. When she was four, it was Cystic Fibrosis induced pancreatitis. At 12, she had to have polyps removed from her nasal cavity. At 16, she developed a serious fungal infection in her lungs. And by 18, she had a small portion of her right lung removed. Not to mention countless bouts of bronchitis and pneumonia in between. It was a bitter feeling to know that she had spent so many months of her life in the hospital just because of one mutated gene.

The elevator jostled to a stop and the doors opened to an all too familiar waiting room covered with rose printed wallpaper.

"Hey, Maggie," Olivia said as she signed in at the nurses' station.

The nurse behind the desk jumped slightly at the sound of her voice but managed to look up with a smile. "Olivia, how are you?"

"Good," she replied and habitually followed Maggie into a nearby alcove equipped with a scale, chair, and blood pressure cuff.

"Let's get this party started," Maggie said with a wink.

This "party" was Olivia's hell, her groundhog day. First, Maggie would check her weight and blood pressure, then take a blood sample. Next, she'd meet with Will, her respiratory therapist, who always managed to find a new problem with her lungs. Then she'd see Jordan, her dietitian, who never felt like she ate enough; followed by Sam, her program therapist, who never thought she was happy enough. And finally, she'd finish with her primary physician, Dr. Katz. All the while, answering the same questions:

Are you keeping up with your physiotherapy?
Are you exercising regularly?
Can you take a deep breath for me?
How many enzyme pills are taking with each meal?

Is your new medication making you feel lightheaded or nauseous?
Can you take a deep breath for me?
How would you describe your current mental state in one word?
How much sleep are you getting each night?
Do you have any chest or stomach pain?
Can you take a deep breath for me?

By the time Olivia wandered back to the nurses' station, she had a pamphlet about the mental and physical benefits of yoga and a serious eye twitch.

"Dr. Katz is running a bit behind," Maggie called to her over the high counter. "Feel free to take a seat while you wait."

Knowing how busy the ward was, "a bit behind" could mean anywhere from fifteen minutes to an hour. Olivia plopped down into a chair in the corner of the waiting room and tried thumbing through an old magazine. But she only watched the pages flip by.

In little over a month, she'll be 28 years old. When she was diagnosed, doctors told her parents that she wouldn't live to see past her 18th birthday. Somehow, she'd made it this far but each passing year gave her more anxiety.

A flicker of light caught the corner of her eye and she looked up to see a twirling mosaic lamp on the other side of the room. It was probably put there to distract wheezing babies while they waited, sticky mucus already weighing heavy on their tiny lungs. The colors danced and flickered around the room, then disappeared when they passed through a harsh ray of sunlight. She stared at the lamp for what felt like hours, trying to bring some peace to her anxious mind.

"Olivia. How are you?"

Her head jerked up to see Dr. Katz walking briskly into the room. His white hair was perfectly parted, not a strand out of place. And, like always, he sported a bowtie and colorful high socks that peeked out below poorly hemmed pants.

"Hi, Dr. Katz." She stood to greet him. "I'm good. How are you?"

"Fine, thank you," he replied quickly before turning and leading her down a long quiet hallway to an examination room.

His socks were the only sign of warmth she'd come to expect. He didn't try to make small talk. Instead, the only sound came from her clicking heels as they passed by overnight rooms. Worn and tired faces peered out at her but Olivia stared straight ahead, not willing to look into the eyes of people just like her.

Dr. Katz took over her case when she turned 18 and moved into the adult program. He was a brilliant and honest man, but also very stoic and cold. She couldn't blame him though. Now in his 60s, it was hard to imagine the number of patients he'd lost to the disease. The problem was: he would never save a patient, just give them more time.

Olivia climbed up onto the examination table and swung her feet nervously. Dr. Katz opened her file and scanned the notes from the day's tests.

"Hmm," he said after a moment.

Hmm? What does 'hmm' mean? Olivia thought as her heart fluttered in her chest. But she quickly pushed the thought away. She was just being paranoid.

Dr. Katz lifted his stethoscope off the back of his neck and placed it on the right side of her chest. "Could you take a deep breath in for me, then let it out slowly?" He moved the stethoscope down and to the right. "One more time?" He looped the stethoscope over the back of his neck once again and nodded. "Let's take a look at your x-rays," he said before rolling his chair over to a computer in the corner of the room.

After a few clicks, he pulled up the images. The lungs glowing on the screen across from her looked a lot like someone had taken white and grey paint and sponged the inside. A normal lung looked clear, with confident white lines striping across the chest. Olivia's, however, had never looked like that and had only gotten blotchier over time.

Dr. Katz sat quietly and massaged his jawline as he stared at the screen. *Why is it taking him so long to speak?* Olivia thought. Her anxiety spiked as if to warn her: *You're getting warmer.*

"That right lung..." he mumbled before turning to face her. "I know we've talked about this in hypotheticals before, but I think it's time we talk seriously about getting you on the lung transplant list."

Olivia's vision blurred as a high-pitch ringing reverberated in her ears and the floor switched places with the ceiling. Panic dripped down her body like ice water and her heart pounded violently in her chest.

"Oh," she whispered. But it was all she could say before her throat closed up like a Venus flytrap.

Dr. Katz walked over to her and put his hand on her shoulder. "I will be here for you every step of the way, no matter what you decide." He looked her square in the eye, sincere and unwavering. For him, it was the equivalent of a hug and pressure started to build behind her eyes.

"What if... What if I don't get the transplant? How long..." her throat tightened again before she could finish.

"It's hard to say," he replied without missing a beat. "Lung infections will be harder to fight off. Gas exchange, in general, will eventually become extremely difficult. It just depends on how much your body is willing to fight. I'd say—"

"—Can I think about it?" she asked. Suddenly, she didn't want to know.

"Of course. I'll have Maggie give you all the information you need: the procedure, risks, costs... but I recommend you make a decision before your next appointment. It can take time to find the right donor."

Olivia nodded, not knowing what else to say. *I'm dying*, she thought, trying to make reality sink in. Granted, she'd been dying since she was diagnosed but now she could actually see the end.

It was as if all her life she'd been locked in a speeding car destined for a cliff, and now she was finally reaching the edge. She knew she would die from this disease yet she'd done nothing to prepare herself. But death waits for no one and her clock was up.

CHAPTER TWO
Jeopardy

A cool breeze cut through the warm air, picking up the edges of her dress. Olivia folded her arms across her chest as she waited at a busy intersection a few blocks away from Warner Theater. Summer had just ended but it was already starting to feel like fall.

A rush hour symphony of honking horns, squeaking bus breaks, and purring engines filled her ears. The light changed and a taxi sped past her, splashing murky water onto her calves.

"Ugh, gross!" she groaned as she tried to shake off the moisture.

Her phone beeped inside her purse and she dug through countless receipts and pill bottles to find it. She was disappointed to see Amanda's name glowing on the screen:

Have fun on your date tonight! Be nice.

Olivia shoved her phone back into her purse. *I'm nice*, she argued silently.

She hadn't told anyone about her conversation with Dr. Katz. When she left the hospital earlier, she thought about calling Ben. His voice alone had the ability to calm her down. But she couldn't bring herself to do it. There was something about saying the words: "I need a lung transplant" out loud that made it that much more real.

Instead, she stupidly let her best friend Amanda talk her into going on a blind date. She was rattled and figured a date would be the perfect distraction from her impending doom.

As if on cue, she was struck by a coughing fit. She doubled over, muffling the sound in the crook of her arm. Evidently, her body was refusing to let her be distracted.

A black Audi with shiny chrome rims pulled up to the curb. "I'm Dan!" the driver yelled over blaring horns reacting to his idled car. "You must be Olivia!"

"Nice to meet you!" she said, a little too aggressively, before slipping into the passenger's seat. Amanda wasn't around but, for some reason, she had a strong urge to prove to her wrong.

Dan had the sun-kissed hair of a devoted surfer and stunning bright hazel eyes. His biceps bulged beneath his fitted shirt enough to show he could probably lift her over his head with one arm.

Olivia raised her eyebrows. *Maybe this wasn't such a bad idea*, she thought.

"Nice place by the way," he said, nodding his head in the direction of a brand new condominium beside them.

"Oh… thanks," she replied, not bothering to explain the complex was just the location of a property she was trying to sell, not her home. The less he knew about her the better, she decided.

They drove to Georgetown and managed to snag a dimly lit table in the heart of a busy Japanese restaurant. The dining room was filled with the laughter and chatter of happy hour regulars. Dan and Olivia's table, however, was filled with a thick, uncomfortable silence.

Okay, this was a bad idea, she decided as they both pretended to examine the restaurant's wallpaper choice. Desperate to do something with her hands, she pulled out a bottle of enzyme pills from her purse.

"Forgot to take my vitamins today," she mumbled. It was a lie, of course, but she wasn't about to tell Dan that she had Cystic Fibrosis and just learned five hours ago that she needed a lung transplant in order to survive. She tossed a handful of pills into her mouth. He didn't even notice.

"So, how's work going?" he asked casually as if they already knew what each other did for a living.

"It's good… I'm a real estate agent working through a small independent agency. So, we're always busy."

Dan nodded. Silence returned. Olivia cringed.

"Um, how about you?" she asked.

"Well, the campaign has been crazy," he said as he leaned forward on his elbows.

Politics? Great. If she knew anything about meeting new people it was that you never brought up politics, religion, or money and they were already discussing one of them.

Dan launched into a story about a senator confusing Slovakia with Slovenia and Olivia immediately glazed over. *Maybe I can get home in time for Jeopardy*, she thought.

"So, have you always lived around here?" Dan asked, breaking Olivia from her trance.

"Yeah, I grew up in Alexandria and went to Maguire University downtown." She decided to leave out the fact that she had to drop out of Maguire before her junior year because Cystic Fibrosis enjoyed ruining her life. "How about you?"

"I'm originally from New York but moved down here about six years ago after I got a job on the Hill." Dan nodded to himself then looked down and started playing with his chopsticks.

Bless this beautiful man but this is painful, Olivia thought. Out of the corner of her eye, she spotted their waiter and waved him down. "Could I get a sake, please?" she asked before he reached their table. "And keep them coming."

Two rolls of sushi and three sakes later, Olivia felt nauseous but much more at ease. She wasn't exactly enjoying the date, but there were no more awkward silences and she actually laughed once.

After dinner, she excused herself and headed to the restroom. She felt pathetic as she breathed in and out of her portable nebulizer barricaded in a bathroom stall. But she didn't feel like seeing the confused faces of whoever decided to visit the women's restroom.

By the time she returned, Dan had already taken care of the check. The sake she had at dinner convinced her to walk down the street with him to a billiards bar. It then convinced her to purchase a pitcher of beer and challenge two Georgetown students to a game of pool. Before long, it was almost 1:00 a.m. and Olivia couldn't hold a pool stick without letting it slide out of her hands and slap against the head of one of her opponents.

Swaying back and forth on their way out of the bar, Dan grabbed her hand and pulled her closer. She leaned into him and for a moment felt wanted and safe.

"Want to go back to my place?" he slurred. "I live nearby."

If he had asked her at the beginning of the night, she might have said yes. But at this point, the alcohol was getting the better her and it felt like she was breathing through a straw. She needed to get home and forget this day.

"I should go… it's late," she said.

Dan looked disappointed but didn't press her. Instead, he leaned in and gave her a wet, sloppy kiss. Olivia felt like the entire bottom half of her face was in his mouth. She gently pushed him away.

"Until next time," he said, then turned and walked away confidently, as if he'd done it a thousand times.

Once out of earshot, Olivia broke into a fit of coughs that she had been holding back. She tried flagging down a taxi, but three passed her without pause.

She pulled out her phone: 1:03 a.m. *Great.* For a moment, she thought about calling out sick from work. But she hadn't missed a day in almost two months and she didn't want to break her streak now.

A taxi slowed and rolled to a stop next to her, crunching gravel under its wheels. She climbed in and gave the driver her address.

As the cab moved forward, Olivia leaned back and tried to take deep breaths but it felt like a heavy weight had been placed on her chest. She coughed again and again, desperate to loosen the mucus in her lungs. Her driver looked back in his mirror disgusted.

"Don't worry, it's not contagious," she said without looking at him.

Ten minutes and a $20 cab fare later, she was back in the comfort of her studio apartment in Adams Morgan. She grabbed a water bottle from the fridge and headed straight to her bed where she found Minkus curled up in a tight ball on top of one of her pillows.

"Hey buddy," she whispered as she rubbed behind his ears. He cooed but didn't lift his head or open his eyes. Even her cat didn't think anyone should be up this late on a weeknight.

Next to her bedside table was a Physiotherapy vest that Amanda nicknamed "Theo." She joked that if Olivia spent half as much time with a real man as she did Theo, she would probably be married with two kids by now.

Olivia strapped on the black vest, connected the tubes, and turned on the machine. She sat on the edge of her bed as the vest began to tighten and shake, beating her lungs to free her airways. She knew that in 20 minutes she would start to feel relief from the constricting mucus filling her lungs. She leaned back against the mountain of pillows next to Minkus, closed her eyes, and gave in to her reality.

CHAPTER THREE
Jelly Donut

The next morning, Olivia found Amanda waiting for her outside the office. Her dark hair was pulled back behind her head in a low bun and she held the world's biggest cup of coffee. As Olivia approached, Amanda's face tightened with worry.

"Are you alright?" she asked.

"I'm fine. Just a long night."

Apparently, Olivia's makeup did nothing to hide how weak and lethargic she felt. Amanda always had the ability to see right through her. After all, they'd known each other for almost six years.

Amanda paused as she processed her response. "You didn't," she finally said and Olivia knew immediately where her mind went.

"I don't know what you mean," she responded coyly and pushed past Amanda toward the front door.

"Haven't you heard of playing hard to get?" Amanda hustled to keep up with her. "I hope he was worth it," she added.

"Can't say he was actually." Olivia looked away to hide her smile. It was too easy.

"Olivia!"

"Okay, okay," she caved. "Nothing happened. In fact, Dan and I will probably never see each other again."

She pushed through a set of double doors and breathed deeply, taking in the familiar scent of Lysol and coffee. She loved her job and was good at it. It was the one area of her life that she hadn't neglected.

"I don't know why you're so afraid of being in a relationship,"

Amanda said. "Love is life's greatest gift."

"Did you get that from a fortune cookie?"

"No, I can attest to it," she argued. "Look at me and Eric."

Olivia stifled a laugh. Amanda wasn't someone who should be preaching about the greatness of love. She had been with her boyfriend, Eric, for three years and a year ago they moved in together. One month into the move, Eric got a "promotion" and ever since has had to go on "business trips" every other week. Now, they saw each other even less and fought even more.

They squeezed through a narrow hallway into a large, simple room with 12 cubicles. Olivia threw her purse down on her desk and immediately started digging through drawers for a forgotten granola bar. She didn't have time to grab breakfast on her way out this morning and her stomach grumbled in protest.

"Look, I don't care what you do with your personal life," Amanda continued as she sat down at her desk. "I just want you to be—"

"Do you have anything to eat?" Olivia asked, cutting her off.

"You need something high in calories," she worthlessly responded. A few WebMD articles on Cystic Fibrosis and she thought she was an expert.

Olivia picked up her stapler and began considering the implications of chucking it at Amanda's face. If there was anyone she loved and hated like a sister, it was Amanda. But before she could wind up her pitch, Amanda's phone rang and she used the distraction to slip away.

Olivia made her way to the kitchen in desperate need of space and food. To her surprise, the kitchen was empty and a big box of donuts sat on one of the lunch tables. Olivia looked up at the ceiling and praised the pastry gods. She needed some alone time with a jelly donut.

She pulled down her favorite oversized mug from the shelf above the coffee maker and grabbed a Coke out of the fridge. As she filled her mug, Amanda walked in with the office assistant, Natalie.

"How did last night go?" Natalie asked as she reached for a pink frosted donut.

Olivia quickly started chugging her soda so she wouldn't pour it over Natalie's head.

"Are you sure you won't go out with him again?" Amanda looked at her curiously.

"Yes, I'm sure."

"What happened?" Natalie asked through a mouthful of donut.

"Olivia. Amanda." Their boss suddenly appeared in the kitchen doorway. "I need to see you both in my office. Now."

Thankful for the interruption, Olivia grabbed a jelly donut and quickly headed for the door. "I'll tell you about it later," she heard Amanda whisper to Natalie before leaving the kitchen.

Sunshine River Burdill, or "Burdi" for short, was a woman Olivia would never question or keep waiting. A true child of the 1960s, the 50-year-old botoxed blonde was someone she'd really come to admire. She was smart, blunt and fiercely independent. After a huge settlement from her first marriage, she opened Sunshine River Properties when she was only 25 years old.

Before Burdi, the future was hard for Olivia to imagine. She always got the impression that, because of her disease, she should find a career and personal life that would ensure success in fast-forward. Burdi had never looked at her like a clock counting down and, for that, she would always be grateful.

They followed Burdi like devoted ducklings past a block of cubicles and into her office. As she took a seat in one of the small leather chairs across from Burdi's desk, Olivia folded over as a wave of coughs ripped through her chest.

"Are you taking care of yourself, Olivia?" Burdi asked sternly. "I can't have you out for weeks at a time again."

"Of course," she replied, hoping her face didn't give anything away. What lung transplant?

Amanda fidgeted in the chair next to her. She'd always been uncomfortable around Burdi and had a hard time hiding it. Burdi, however, enjoyed her discomfort and stared at her intently.

"How's Bruce?" Olivia asked, hoping it would draw her attention away from Amanda.

Burdi continued to stare. "Madly in love with me, of course."

"Do I hear wedding bells?" Amanda blurted out.

Olivia suddenly got the urge to slap her forehead. Burdi had already been through two failed marriages and she and Bruce had only been dating for a few months.

"Don't insult me, Amanda," Burdi retorted then quickly changed the subject. "I'm doing something a little different with our company holiday party this year." She paused as if she was waiting for a drum roll. "It's going to be on New Year's Eve! Picture it: 100 people in cocktail attire, music, and champagne. We've been in business for 25 years now so it's only appropriate, don't you think?" She clapped her hands together in excitement.

"Where are we going to find 100 people?" Amanda asked. With only 16 people in the entire company, it was a fair question. But Olivia sent Amanda her best side-eye anyway.

"I want you two to help me plan it," Burdi continued.

Amanda stiffened and Olivia was sure she looked just as surprised. "I don't know anything about event planning," Olivia said.

"That's okay," Burdi reassured her. "I just need people I can trust to make this happen."

Olivia took a bite of her donut to buy herself more time while Amanda just sat there with her mouth open. She watched Burdi's face as she absentmindedly bent a paperclip out of shape, waiting for them to respond. There was a hint of desperation in her eyes.

"Of course we'll help you," she finally said.

"I'd be honored!" Amanda exclaimed.

Olivia fought the urge to roll her eyes.

"Thank you," Burdi said with a sigh. "I'll get the first planning meeting on our calendars." She pulled open a file on her desk and started highlighting. After a moment, she looked up and acted surprised to see them still sitting there. "You can leave now."

Amanda and Olivia didn't hesitate. They both rose and practically ran into each other as they hustled out the door.

"What just happened?" Amanda asked once they were a full a cubicle length from Burdi's office. "Did I just give up my New Year's Eve plans to spend forced, quality time with my boss?"

"What New Year's Eve plans, Miss I'd be honored!"

"I was terrified."

"She needs our help."

"She needs help alright..." Amanda mumbled.

"She doesn't have many friends. I think we should make an effort."

"She's my boss. Not my friend. Those lines shouldn't cross."

"They're about to," Olivia teased.

"I'm ignoring you now." She plopped down in front of her desk but couldn't hide her smile.

Olivia laughed as she gathered up a stack of open house flyers. Her phone dinged and she looked down to see a text message from Dan:

I'm still thinking about that kiss from last night. ☺ We should do it again soon.

Olivia deleted the text and tossed her phone into her bag. She needed another donut.

CHAPTER FOUR
The Dogwood Tree

It was dark by the time Olivia pulled up to the 1940s brick colonial. A warm glow slipped through the curtains on the first floor and cascaded across the front lawn. She knew her father was anxiously awaiting her arrival on the other side of those walls: tasting the pasta sauce, straightening a napkin, checking his watch. Wash, rinse, repeat.

On her way up the driveway, she passed a dogwood tree, dry and limp after the harsh summer months. And she knew it had only survived this long because her father painstakingly poured over its survival just as he had hers.

It had been her mother's favorite tree. She planted it just after Olivia was born. For her, it stood as a testament to miracles because at thirty-seven she had almost given up on her dream of ever having children.

"This tree is just as old as you, Olivia. Care for it and it will never die." Olivia could still hear her voice. And if she closed her eyes she could still see her sitting under that tree, soaking up the warm rays of the sun, light shining through her golden hair and the smile of a movie star.

But just as quickly as the memory came it vanished. The cool night air replaced the warm sun and she found herself standing in the dark, cold and alone. Her father always said that she gave her mother the best years of her life. But Olivia couldn't help but think she had helped her to her grave.

She took a deep breath as she climbed the back porch steps to the house. "Don't think. Just tell him," she whispered to herself before pushing open the door.

Almost immediately, she was hit by a warm, savory smell. Ever since her mother died, her father was forced to be a jack-of-all-trades. Whether it was the "the birds and the bees" talk or shopping for her prom dress, he stepped up to the plate. Recently, he had taken an interest in cooking. It was never his strength but Ben helped him go from burnt grilled cheese to a decent roast chicken.

"Dad?"

"Hey, honey!" Her father called from the kitchen. "I'm elbow-deep in mashed potatoes! Be out in a minute!"

Olivia tossed her purse over to the couch in the other room, narrowly missing Teddy Roosevelt, her father's Jack Russell terrier. "Woops. Sorry, Teddy," she mumbled. Teddy simply snorted at her then rested his head back down on his paws.

The house hadn't changed since her mother's death. The décor consisted of an eclectic mix of thrift store finds and family pass-downs. Every inch was covered with some kind of trinket but it still managed to be warm and inviting.

Her eyes landed on a picture taken before her first day of kindergarten. Her mother stood behind her with her arms wrapped around her small shoulders. She had the biggest grin on her face.

Olivia smiled, remembering the moment. She had been terrified that the other kids would make fun of her for all the pills she had to take. Just before the picture was taken, her mother had put hair in braids and said: "Baby, how could anyone make fun of you? With those beautiful indigo eyes, that perfect smile, and most importantly…" She'd paused and pointed to her chest, "…such a kind heart?"

"Good to see you, baby girl."

Olivia dragged her gaze away from the picture to greet her father. He was shorter than her and balding, with a large nose and soft features. A blue frilly apron was tied around his waist, covering his sweater vest and khakis. Minus the apron, it was rare for her to ever see him without this ensemble during a weekday—as if it was the required uniform for high school history teachers everywhere.

"Hi, Dad."

He pulled her in for a hug and she was immediately hit by the familiar smell of his strong, earthy cologne. "How are you? How did your appointment go yesterday?"

Olivia's anxiety spiked. She'd hoped to ease into the conversation but wasn't surprised her father asked so quickly. He was a worrier by nature and the more information he had, the more he felt like he might be in control. She hesitated as she tried to find a way to slow it all down.

"Fine. The usual," she said with a shrug. "He's concerned about my right lung."

"I can't remember a time when he wasn't concerned about that lung," he replied.

Olivia shuffled her hands like a deck of cards. She didn't want to lie to him but was keeping something from him lying? His eyes pierced into her as if he knew there was more.

"Dad…" she paused to take a deep breath. "He thinks it's time." She knew that was all she needed to say for her father to understand.

His face fell almost instantly. Olivia was pretty sure she just witnessed his appetite disappear. He looked down at his shoes and nodded.

"Okay." His voice shook. "Have you made a decision yet?"

"No… but you'll be the first to know."

He nodded again and looked back up at her. "I thought I'd be more prepared for this."

Olivia smiled weakly. "Me too."

"I love you, honey. Whatever you need…" his voice cracked.

"I know," she assured him.

He cleared his throat and turned away. Even when her mother died, he refused to let her see him cry. "Dinner's almost ready," he said, quickly changing the subject. "Interested in some wine?"

She sighed. "I'll take a bottle."

Olivia leaned back in her chair and gulped down the rest of her Cabernet. She was so full that she felt like her stomach was going to burst. This time she didn't have to fake loving the meal. Her father really did get it right.

"That was delicious, Dad. Thank you."

"You should really be thanking Ben. He taught me everything I know!" he said proudly.

"I'll try to do that," she murmured without meeting his eyes. Olivia thought about how that conversation might go: *Hey Ben! So, I had dinner with my dad the other night. Wanted to tell you: great meatloaf. Also… I need a lung transplant.*

"I'm going to visit Mom this weekend," her father said, interrupting her thoughts. "There are some sunflowers in the backyard I think I'll bring her. You know, they're her fav—"

"Her favorite flower. I know."

Olivia looked down and played with some scraps on her plate. Her father had a habit of feeding her facts about her mother in casual conversation. He assumed that Olivia didn't remember her quirks and interests since she was only seven when she died. Little did he know, the memories she had of her mother played in loops, over-and-over again in her head.

"Would you like to come with me?"

"No," she replied curtly but quickly regretted it. She gave him a half-hearted smile, hoping it would soften the blow.

Her father visited her mother's grave every week. As a religious man, it was his way of being close to her again. But it wasn't how Olivia remembered her, so going would never put her at ease.

"I miss her," she said.

"Me too." He looked over at her mother's empty seat at the table.

Olivia reached for his hand and gave it a gentle squeeze. He squeezed back but refused to peel his gaze away from her chair. She could tell that was the end of their conversation.

✳ ✳ ✳

Olivia threw a mushy fry to a pigeon as Amanda furiously typed away on her phone. The two sat at a picnic table in a small neighborhood park a few blocks away from their office.

"You have to get a bilateral lung transplant? As in both?"

"Yeah, to prevent infection," Olivia replied. "Look, I don't even know if I'll do it. It's an expensive surgery and not even a solution." But it was useless. Amanda was already knee deep in her Google research.

"What if you made a pro-con list?" Amanda asked, without looking away from her phone.

Olivia humored her and thought for a moment. *Pro: I might survive the transplant surgery; con: I'll die… this isn't helping.*

"Jeez, you have to take a lot of tests to even get approved for a transplant," she mumbled.

Olivia sighed and pushed a dead leaf off the wooden picnic table. She had read through all the materials Dr. Katz had given her a dozen times but she still didn't know what to do.

Amanda reached across the table and took her hand. "Olivia, whatever you need..."

"I know." She smiled and squeezed her hand.

Olivia's phone buzzed against the wooden table. She turned it toward her and saw Ben's name flash on the screen.

"Have you told him?" Amanda asked, peeking at her phone.

"No, not yet. I've been avoiding him actually." Ben was the first person she wanted to talk to but the last person she wanted to tell.

"Oh." Amanda raised her eyebrows.

"What?"

"Nothing. It's not important right now."

"If we played by those rules then all we'd talk about is the lung transplant. Spill."

"Pete called me yesterday. Ben and Molly broke up."

"What? When?" She was shocked. They had just moved in together.

"I don't know the details," Amanda continued as she stirred her chocolate milkshake. "Just that they broke it off a week ago and Ben's been hiding out in his condo ever since."

A week ago? Olivia suddenly felt guilty about avoiding him.

Amanda shook her head. "I really thought Molly might be the one."

"I didn't."

"In her defense, what woman is going to be okay with her boyfriend hanging out with his ex-girlfriend all the time?"

"We never dated."

"So you say." She gave Olivia a sideways glance before picking up her phone again.

Olivia decided it was better not to argue. Instead, she looked down at Ben's message still glowing unread on the screen. Her heart started to pound just looking at it. *Why am I so nervous?* she thought. *It's just Ben.*

CHAPTER FIVE
Naked Boy

I'm free! Olivia thought as she walked down the steps in front of Stewart Hall. It was mid-way through the spring semester of her freshman year and she was just leaving a grueling biology mid-term.

Exhausted, she began making her way across the dewy lawn with a stack of biology books in her arms. She took a deep breath, filling her lungs with the fresh, cool air. Nearly a year ago to the day she had part of her right lung removed and it felt so good to breathe easy. Well, easier.

As she walked, she wrestled with her thoughts: *I don't want to go… Alright fine, I'll go… but I'm so tired… okay maybe just for a little while.*

She couldn't decide whether or not she had the energy to go to the Pi Kappa Alpha initiation party that night. One of the brothers she sat next to in Biology had invited her and according to her roommate, Beth, that was a "big freaking deal" and she'd better go.

Distant laughter and whooping made its way across the courtyard from students who had already started Greek initiation festivities. The carefree sound came bouncing through the campus buildings, begging her to join in on the fun.

"Alright, I'm going," she said out loud, thinking it would cement her decision.

The laughter quickly got louder and the whooping much more pronounced. Olivia looked around for its source but couldn't see much in the thick darkness. She picked up her pace and made a sharp turn toward the middle of campus.

Suddenly, a herd of 12 sprinting men rushed toward her. She tried to get out of the way but ended up directly in the path of one of the runners. They collided with a loud smack. Olivia's books went flying across the lawn as she stumbled backward and landed hip-to-hip under a toned and tall man with beautiful brown eyes.

"I am so sorry! Are you okay?" he shouted in her face, clearly intoxicated. She got a strong whiff of whiskey as his hot breath brushed her cheeks.

"I'm alright," she squeaked.

He rolled off her and lifted her up off the ground by her elbows. After a few vicious coughs Olivia looked up at him. *Oh, God*, she thought. He's completely naked.

"I'm Ben," he said casually and handed her one of her books.

It took all she had to keep her eyes focused on his face. "Olivia." She took the book from him. "You're naked."

"I am." He smiled and pushed his chest out with pride. "It's my last night pledging and this was our final requirement... err optional requirement."

"Right. Well, congratulations. This seemed like a successful streak."

"As long as I don't get arrested."

Olivia smiled awkwardly as she bent down to pick up the last book. "That's a lot of books," he said, staring at the stack she'd gathered.

"Mid-terms," she responded with a shrug.

He looked around. "Damn, I don't know where the others ran off to. I hate to cut this short but I've got to go."

Another fit of coughs hit Olivia and she turned away embarrassed.

"You sure you're okay?" he asked and took a step toward her. "I hit you pretty hard."

She waved him off. "Yeah, don't worry. Happens all the time."

"Lucky you," he said with a wink.

They smiled at each other for a moment. He was a naked stranger, inches away from her, but there was a pull in her gut begging her to stay close to him.

"See you around, Olivia." He took off running again and she watched his glowing backside fade away into the darkness.

"I just want a beer!" she shouted inaudibly over the thumping bass. Olivia had been waiting to get to the PKA bar since she arrived and desperately needed a drink to calm her nerves. The crowd in the frat house was so dense her arms had to stay permanently pinned at her side. One more body and she was pretty sure the floorboards would cave in.

She finally managed to push her way forward and claimed a spot at the handmade wooden bar top. Leaning over the table, she attempted to make eye contact with the PKA brother handing out drinks.

"Hey, beautiful. Beer or jungle juice?"

"Beer."

He pumped the tap and filled her cup with the golden liquid. She grabbed her drink and did a 180 to find Sam, who she last saw standing next to a crumbling fireplace decorated with Christmas lights.

WHAM! She slammed into something hard. The wind was knocked out of her and she gasped for air. Half of her drink spilled, leaving her white t-shirt soaked and see-through.

"Fantastic," she said.

"Whoa, library girl! Two times in one night!" Ben stood over her smiling.

"Naked boy," she grumbled. "Always a pleasure."

Olivia started shaking her drenched shirt to get it dry but then gave up. She looked up at Ben. They were wedged close enough together that she could see the details of his face. He had dark, golden skin, a sharp jawline covered in just a hint of stubble, and flecks of gold scattered across his brown eyes. She had to admit: Ben was adorable.

"Let me guess, you're pledging PKA?" she yelled above the music.

"Pledged. You're looking at a proud brother now!"

The crowd around them became even denser. She was forced to shuffle closer to Ben's lean, muscular frame until they were pressed up against each other much like earlier—only this time they were vertical. The top of her head reached just below his chin. And she could tell he didn't know what to do with his hands. He kept putting one on her lower back then removing it again. But every time he touched her, she felt a tingle of nervousness in her stomach that wasn't all that unpleasant.

He leaned toward her, studying her face. Their mouths were inches apart, breathing the same air. Olivia's heart began to pound.

"I'm sorry, I can't help but notice: your shirt is see-through!" he yelled.

She tipped her head back and laughed. "That's because you spilled my beer all over me!"

At that very moment, someone pushed past her and she spilled the rest of her beer all over Ben. She grabbed his forearms for support to keep herself from falling over.

"Now look who's spilling beer," he said in her ear.

"I'm so sorry!" She looked down and saw that her hands were still glued to his forearms and quickly broke her grasp.

"Hey, no sweat. I'll get you another." He cupped his hands over his mouth and shouted to the bartender: "Yo, Drew! Can I get two beers over here?"

In a matter of seconds, two beers were passed overhead to Ben. He carefully lowered one into Olivia's hand.

"Wow, where were you 10 minutes ago?"

"Stick with me. I'll take care of you."

Just like before, they stared at each other for a moment. Ben's hand had found her lower back again but this time it stayed. The heat from his touch burned through to her skin.

This is crazy, she thought and looked down at her feet. "Actually, I should probably go," she said and took a painful step back.

"Where? The library?" he asked with a crooked grin.

"Haha," she said, dragging out a fake laugh. "No, I should go find Sam." She pointed in the direction of the fireplace. "He invited me tonight and I told him I'd come find him after I got a drink."

"You came here with Sam O'Connell?" His brow furrowed.

"Technically, I met him here."

"Lucky guy." His eyes shifted away from hers.

"What?" Olivia shouted over the music.

"Nothing," he shrugged. "Have a great night."

He smiled but Olivia could tell he was disappointed. And, honestly, she was too. Deep down, she wanted to stay but was terrified of how she felt around him.

"I'm sure we'll run into each other again," she said before squeezing her way through the crowd.

"I'll look for you in the library!" he shouted after her.

"Just promise me you'll wear clothes!" she shouted back.

He laughed and lifted his red solo cup to her. As she walked away, the feeling he gave her and the warmth of his touch stayed with her.

CHAPTER SIX
The Rat Tail

The memory of how Olivia first met Ben came flooding back to her as she walked into O'Brien's Pub. Shiny mahogany covered the galley style bar from floor to ceiling and a four-piece band played on a tiny, raised stage in the back. The chaotic activity and pulsing music in the packed bar reminded her of college and she was quickly consumed by warm nostalgia.

She was late because she needed time with her physiotherapy vest and the already congested bar made her journey to find her friends difficult. By the time she made it to the back where the band was in the middle of "Wild Rover," she had to creatively maneuver her way around patrons singing and swaying.

After ducking under one particularly enthusiastic man's elbow, she spotted Ben sitting in a corner booth. Their eyes locked instantly and Olivia froze. For a moment she forgot to breathe. He looked almost exactly as he did in college, only with a little more meat on his bones and harder features around his face.

Ben smiled and waved to her in an attempt to break her frozen state. A nervous electrical charge shot through her body making her heart flutter. She forced her feet forward but it felt like she was walking through mud.

"Nice of you to join us," Pete said with a sideways grin.

"Sorry I'm late." She plopped down next to Ben.

"It's been a while," he said, looking down at her under his arm.

His warm breath brushed against her cheeks and his deep brown eyes had her transfixed. She could feel herself leaning into him as if he had some kind of magnetic pull on her.

"You got here just in time," Amanda called from across the table. "Pete just ordered—"

"—Irish Car Bombs, baby!" Pete shouted.

Amanda looked at him as if she'd like to set him on fire with her eyes.

"It's the only way I know how to get this guy out of his funk," he continued. "That, and you of course." He winked at Olivia, his green eyes shadowed with mischief.

"Happy to help," Olivia replied. She refused to let Pete's comments make tonight awkward. Throughout the years she'd known him, Pete had made it no secret that he thought the two of them should crawl into bed together.

"I haven't been in a funk," Ben corrected. "I've been working on a business plan for a restaurant."

"Ben, I think it's important to grieve," Amanda said softly.

"What did you say?" Pete stared at Ben, his eyes bright.

"I'm looking for a partner," Ben said. "Interested?"

"Are you serious?"

"I'm serious! I really need your money," he deadpanned.

"I'm in!" Pete exclaimed and the two slapped hands across the table, making it official.

"What made you finally decide to do it?" Olivia asked.

Since the day she met him, Ben had always talked about owning his own restaurant. At the time, he was a line cook at a local diner. He got his degree in business from Maguire to please his father but right after graduating he enrolled in culinary school. To help pay the bills, he took a job at an upscale French restaurant where he met Pete. The two never stopped talking about what they would do if they ever owned a restaurant.

"I don't know." He shrugged. "It just feels like the right time."

"Well, I think it's great. I'm proud of you." She smiled up at him.

"Thanks," he said and dropped his arm around her shoulders. "You can help us find the real estate, right?"

"Of course."

Their waitress appeared with a tray of drinks. She leaned over the table and sent Pete a coy smile before walking away.

"You've slept with our waitress, haven't you?" Amanda narrowed her eyes at Pete.

29

"How do you think we snagged such a good table?" he replied and Amanda's mouth fell open in shock. "Well, I can think of no better way to celebrate this moment," Pete continued as he pulled his Irish Car Bomb closer.

"I don't know if I can do this," Amanda said looking at the shot and Guinness in front of her. "My chugging days are long gone."

"You never had any," Pete mumbled before starting again. "A toast…" He held up his shot. "To the restaurant. May these drinks be the first of many we drink in its honor!"

The four leaned forward and clinked their glasses together.

"And the first person to finish gets to name the restaurant," Pete added quickly before dropping his shot into his pint glass.

Olivia scrambled to tip her glass up to her lips. The thick stout rushed to the back of her throat and coated the lining of her stomach as it went down, warming her from the inside out. She slammed her glass down on the table with a single dry cough only to find that she had finished third. Amanda, however, was still only halfway through.

"Hurry up!" Pete yelled.

"I'm doing the best I can!" she protested, breaking her chug.

"Don't stop!" he said through laughter.

Amanda's face was flushed and she sported a dripping Guinness mustache. "Oh, forget it!" She shoved her glass into Pete's hands who gladly finished it off for her.

"So who won?"

"Olivia, do you seriously doubt my abilities?" Pete looked at her feigning surprise.

"Best out of three!" Ben challenged.

"Nobody likes a sore loser, Ben. And I personally think *The Rat Tail* will be an excellent name."

"Okay, we're definitely going again," Ben said and looked around for their waitress.

"Not me," Amanda peeped.

"Same," Olivia agreed. She was starting to feel nauseous. Apparently, she didn't learn her lesson from her night out with Dan.

"Are you okay?" Ben asked, giving her a gentle nudge.

That's a loaded question, she thought. "I'm fine," she said instead.

"Tonight's ending in karaoke," Pete announced.

"No!" Amanda and Olivia shouted in unison.

Ben pointed one finger up, over his head and down again like he was in the Grease Lightning music video. "This one is for that girl right over there... in the corner, pretending to ignore me. Yeah, that one. This one's for you."

The crowd swooned but Olivia shook her head and smiled. It wasn't the first time Ben had publically dedicated a song to her while in an intoxicated state.

Pete started to play a sloppy version of "I Got You Babe" on the piano and the two did their best impressions of Sonny and Cher. A smile played on Olivia's lips as she watched Ben stomp his foot and dip the mic stand toward the crowd.

An alarm went off on Olivia's phone and she reluctantly pulled her gaze away from the performance to silence it. When she turned, she saw Amanda staring at her.

"What?" she asked as she pulled out her pillbox and popped a colorful concoction into her mouth.

"Nothing," she replied unconvincingly.

"Suit yourself," Olivia said through a mouthful of pills before swallowing.

"Oh, just go for it," Amanda caved. "What do you have to lose?"

"What are you talking about?"

"You know what I'm talking about." She flicked her head in Ben's direction.

"No."

"Why?"

"What makes you think I can handle a committed relationship? I can barely breathe—the one thing that comes most naturally to people."

"So you're just going to sit in your comfortable little box and just... survive?"

"Yeah, I'm actually pretty happy when I make it through the day alive."

Amanda crossed her arms, her lips set in a hard line. Olivia knew what she was thinking but also knew she would never say it: *Stop using your disease as an excuse.*

It was true though. Olivia always used her disease as the reason for not doing something outside of her comfort zone. But in her opinion, it was a lot easier to "live like you're dying" when you weren't actually dying.

"I'm sorry," Olivia said as she rubbed her eyes. "It's been a hell of a week."

"I know," Amanda replied despondently.

"Look, even if I wanted to, Ben and I can't be together," she continued, despite her internal struggle. "I care about him too much."

"Okay, now try *not* using a cliché."

"You wouldn't like my answer."

"Try me."

On one hand, Olivia had been alone for so long that the idea of suddenly sharing her life with someone else sounded terrifying. But she knew that wouldn't be a good enough reason for Amanda. It wasn't even a good enough reason for her. Instead, she decided to give a reason that Amanda, of all people, would understand.

"Our story wouldn't end in happily ever after. It would end in disaster. We'd barely have a life together. There's no rewriting it. I'm just waiting for the day my body decides to give up which, now, might be sooner than later."

"You're right. I don't like it," she said and looked down at her drink.

"Please understand… I just won't be around for as long as he deserves."

"I do. I hear you," she said gently. "But have you ever considered the pain you're putting him through by not giving him a chance?"

"There's another person out there for him. He just needs to let himself see that."

"Now, *that* I don't agree with."

"You don't have to."

"Fine, but one more question." She leaned forward on her elbows. "Are you in love with him?"

"It doesn't matter," Olivia mumbled.

"Actually, it does. Don't count yourself out, Olivia. You deserve happiness too."

Before she could respond, the crowd began clapping and singing along with Ben as he made his way off the stage and over to their table. He slid into the booth and belted the final lines.

I got you to kiss goodnight
I got you to hold me tight
I got you, I won't let go
I got you to love me so

He held Olivia with one arm and the microphone with the other. They swayed back-and-forth in the booth as the crowd looked on and she felt a rush of heat fill her cheeks. When the song ended, the crowd cheered and Ben placed a gentle kiss on her temple.

How could she not be in love with this man? The truth was: Ben had a permanent hold on her heart. She was in love with him and had been since the day they met.

CHAPTER SEVEN
One Hell of a Memory

They finally managed to drag Ben and Pete away from the stage and out of the bar just before last call. Much to Amanda's annoyance, her shoulder acted as a crutch for Pete who kept making kissing noises in her ear.

"I swear, I'm going to punch you in the face if you don't knock it off," she said through clenched teeth.

"Ya know… you're a really pprrretty lady when you're hair issss down." He began twirling a piece of her hair around his finger.

Amanda stared at him for a moment then turned to Olivia. "I'm going to find him a cab. Can you walk Ben home?"

Olivia looked at Ben who was staring intently at the night sky. Luckily, he hadn't had nearly as much to drink as Pete. "Yeah, text me when you get home."

"It might be a while." She looked at Pete who was now nestling his head against her shoulder. "Depends on how long it takes me to bury the body."

Olivia laughed and forced Ben into an about-face. They walked arm-and-arm like they had been doing it for years. She leaned against him, taking comfort in the silence and his warm skin.

"I like this," he said.

"Walking?" she teased.

"Being with you."

Olivia's cheeks burned and she looked down at her feet. "I'm sorry it didn't work out with Molly," she said to change the subject.

"It wasn't meant to be. I'm in love with someone else." He looked down at her and panic immediately began to build in her chest.

"I need a lung transplant," she blurted out and pulled away from him.

"What?" His face went pale.

"I just found out."

He was quiet for a moment as he rubbed the back of his neck. "You're going to get it… right?"

"I haven't decided yet," she said.

"Ben I—"

Before she could finish, he grabbed her hand and pulled her across the street to a dark alley. The faint sound of Jazz music reached them from the basement of a nearby brick building. He wrapped his hands around the first bar of a rusty fire escape and started to climb.

"What are you doing? We need to talk!" Olivia shouted up at him.

"That's exactly what we need to stop doing," he called down to her. "Come on."

"Are you out of your mind? Get down here before you get arrested!" She looked around to see if they had attracted any attention.

"ALL BY MYSELFFFFF! DON'T WANT TO BEEE ALL BY MYSELFFFF!!"

"ALRIGHT! I'm coming! Now please shut up!"

"Wet blanket."

"I heard that," she said as she cautiously put her hands on the cold metal bars.

"Meant for you to."

She shook her head but couldn't help but smile. "What are we doing exactly?"

"Creating one hell of a memory."

When Olivia reached the top, her chest was tight and she was breathing heavily. Ben helped her over the roof's ledge and as her feet hit the rooftop, she burst into a fit of coughs.

"I'm sorry, Olivia. I didn't think…"

"No, no I'm fine." She took a deep breath and look around. "Oh…"

"What did I tell you?" Ben stretched both arms out to the side. "One hell of a memory."

Olivia was speechless as she spun around to take in the 360-degree view. From the Potomac to the Washington Monument, she could see nearly every Washington D.C. landmark in one spot. City lights sparkled around them and cars moved like ants in the distance. The moon was full and golden and the street lamps below created a soft glow, nestling the view into one spectacular backdrop.

"It's beautiful."

Ben stepped closer and took her hands in his. "Dance with me?"

She laughed. "Dance? You don't know how to dance."

Ben ignored her and drew her closer. "Sure I do." He started to sway and clumsily pull her around to an imaginary beat. They weren't in synch at all and looked more like they were in an intimate tug of war.

"I'm the one who's supposed lead."

"I'm letting you lead!" she argued. "And don't you dare step on my toes."

"I would never."

"PKA Spring Formal. Your junior year."

"I wasn't that bad."

"My feet were bruised for weeks!"

"Would you relax? You're ruining the moment," he whispered into her ear, sending a pleasant shiver down her spine.

"Sorry," she whispered back as a smile played on her lips.

Ben hugged her tighter. She relaxed in his arms and rested her head on his chest. She let her eyes close and soon felt her worries slip away. All she could see—past, present, and future—was right there in this moment with Ben.

He pressed his lips against her hair and she pulled back to look at him. The alcohol had faded from his eyes but was still on his breath. He touched her cheek and she leaned into it, taking in every bit of its warmth and comfort. His other hand found her opposite cheek and he leaned in slowly.

Olivia's head was begging her to pull away but her heart won and she met him in a kiss. Their lips pressed together gently. But emotion quickly took over. Pressure and desire increased. His mouth opened and she took the invitation gratefully, gliding her tongue across his lower lip.

"I love you," he whispered through the kiss.

Olivia's heart backed down and her mind started to take the lead. She panicked and stepped back from his arms. "I'm sorry I can't do this." She turned away just as she felt pressure building behind her eyes.

"Why not?"

"You just got out of a relationship. How can you possibly feel that way?"

"I've always loved you, Olivia. We can't be apart, don't you see it?" He ran his hand through his dark hair.

"And being together solves everything? You do realize I come with an expiration date."

"I don't care. I love the way I feel when I'm around you. Everything is better with you."

Olivia's heart was beating so fast it felt as if it was going to explode. She looked up at the sky hoping gravity would stop her tears. Ben took a step closer.

"Please, give us a chance. I don't want to hear all the reasons why you don't think we should be together. I love you and will take care of you. Isn't that enough?"

Olivia stared at him, not knowing what to say. Looking back, she could admit that their lives were constantly intertwined as if the universe had been pushing them together over and over again. Only, she was never willing to take the chance. Their first meeting was just the start of relentlessly shattering Ben's heart. Now, as she looked at him almost 10 years later, she was starting to realize that she had been breaking her own heart too.

Amanda's voice rang in her ears: *Don't count yourself out, Olivia. You deserve happiness too.*

Ben, crumbling under her silence, threw his hands in the air. "I LOVE OLIVIA HAMMEL!" He looked down at her with desperation in his eyes. "Olivia, I'm literally shouting my love for you on a rooftop. What more do you want from me?"

Tears pooled along her bottom eyelashes but a laugh escaped her. Relief filled his face and he grabbed her shoulders.

"My God, woman, what's going on in that head of yours? Let me in!"

"I love you too," she whispered, finally giving in to her heart.

She felt light and giddy like a heavy weight had been lifted off her shoulders. She wrapped her arms around his neck before diving into another mind-numbing kiss. She wasn't thinking and it was the best idea she'd had in a long time.

CHAPTER EIGHT
Peanut Butter Pancakes

A sliver of blurry light peeked through Olivia's eyelids but she squeezed them shut. Last night was amazing but she was paying for it this morning. Her head throbbed and her body ached.

After a moment, she gave in and sat up. Across the room, in a cardboard box, a picture of Ben and Molly came into focus. Olivia shot up from the bed like it was on fire and immediately folded over from a fit of morning coughs. She quickly crossed the cool wooden floor to the bathroom and could feel Molly's eyes on her as she went.

Olivia splashed her face with cold water and stared into the mirror. It suddenly felt wrong to be here. She didn't expect to see some of Molly's belongings still in Ben's condo. It was as if her story had overlapped with another. When she woke up, everything was perfect but now she couldn't be more confused.

As soon as she was dressed, she made her way out of the bedroom where she found the hallway walls covered with more pictures of Ben and Molly. *This puts an interesting twist on the "walk of shame,"* she thought. Her stomach flipped and her mind raced with doubt.

Music drifted down the hall. It got louder and louder, just as her heart pounded faster and faster. When she reached the kitchen, she spotted Ben along with another pile of moving boxes stacked by the door. Only gym shorts covered Ben's body, muscles at the ready.

She followed the line of his spine to the rim of his blue shorts. *What was I worried about again?* she thought.

Olivia took a deep breath to compose herself and instantly became aware of the tight squeeze in her chest. She'd have to get to Theo soon.

"Good morning!" she yelled above the music.

"Hey!" Ben reached for the dial on the sound system hanging from one of the cabinets. "I was wondering when you were going to get up."

Olivia smiled and shrugged, trying not to look distracted by his half-naked body. She climbed up onto a stool at the breakfast bar and found her purse on the seat next to her. She grabbed her pillbox and shook out the concoction she needed.

"I've got chocolate chip pancakes, side of bacon, and, of course, peanut butter and syrup," Ben said as he presented her with an array of plates.

"How'd you know my perfect breakfast?"

"Lucky guess," he said with a wink.

"I like what you've done with the place. The pictures are lovely," Olivia said sarcastically as she spread peanut butter on her pancakes.

"Did you notice the giant one behind you?" he asked.

She swiveled around to see a framed picture the size of any football fanatic's big screen TV above the fireplace. Ben and Molly were both wearing white and sitting cuddled up on a beach. A yelp escaped her before she could stop it.

"I know," Ben said shaking his head. "Neither of us wants any of the pictures now. What a waste."

"Is she still…"

"No," he replied, reading her mind. "She's been staying at a friend's until she can find a place."

Olivia sighed in relief and took a big bite of bacon. Without having to ask, Ben poured her a glass of orange juice and she took her pills with the juice.

"I really am sorry about you and Molly."

"Not your fault."

"It isn't?"

"No, it's not. It would have ended eventually. I never really loved her." He paused and shook his head. "As bad as it sounds: I settled."

"We might have jumped into this a little fast," Olivia said after a beat.

"We've known each other for almost 10 years, Olivia. I don't think so."

"You know what I mean."

"I don't regret anything about last night. Do you?"

"No… maybe just the timing of it."

Ben's eyes locked on the picture behind her. "You're right," he said before turning and flipping a pancake. "Sooner would have been better."

Olivia smiled and shook her head. "So, what now?"

"Go out with me."

She snorted through a mouthful of pancakes. "What?"

He leaned his arms over the counter. "A real date. Just you and me."

"Isn't that a little backward? Aren't you supposed to woo me *before* you sleep with me?"

"Backwards, forwards… doesn't matter to me. I've got a lot of time to make up for."

Her face flushed. "Okay, but only if you burn that thing." she pointed to the giant picture behind her.

"Deal." He smiled and grabbed a sponge. "Hey, if you're done with that dish, go ahead and pass it over."

Olivia gathered her bacon plate and walked around the counter to hand it to Ben.

"Personal delivery?" He took it from her and dropped it into the sink.

"My arms are short and that island is so big," she joked.

Olivia turned to walk back to her seat but Ben caught her wrist. He leaned in and rested his forehead on hers. His aftershave tingled her nose and his warm breath swept across her cheeks. Their lips played against one another before finally giving into a kiss.

In one quick motion, Ben's hands slid to her upper thighs and he lifted her onto the kitchen counter. She could feel her body temperature rise as her heart pounded faster. With one of his hands on the back of her head and the other slowly making its way down her chest, Olivia felt like she was going explode. She wrapped one leg around him as his mouth made its way down her neck. She tilted her head back in delight.

Suddenly, there was the jingling of keys followed by the front door breaking free of its frame. Ben stepped back from the counter to look and Olivia tumbled off, barely catching herself before hitting the tile floor.

Molly stood in the doorway. She stared at the pair as she tried to make sense of what she was seeing. "Olivia. What are you doing here?"

At the sight of her, Olivia immediately felt self-conscious. Molly's red hair was perfectly in place and her skin practically glowed, while

Olivia probably had eyeliner smudged down to her cheek.

"I thought you weren't stopping by until this afternoon?" Ben leaned a shoulder against the fridge.

Molly continued to look back-and-forth between the two of them. "I *was* right," she said just barely above a whisper and threw her enormous beige purse down on the couch.

"Olivia's helping me find a space for my restaurant," Ben replied quickly.

The air flew from Olivia's lungs like a punch to the gut. Just last night he was shouting that he loved her on a rooftop and now she was just his realtor.

"So, you're actually going to do it?" Molly said in disbelief. "I never thought I'd see the day," she added, almost incoherently, before turning to a stack of boxes.

"Why not? Pete and I have always talked about it and this is the perfect time to—"

"—You and Pete?" She laughed without humor and hoisted a box into her arms. "You'll definitely succeed then."

"Well, we don't plan on just *going through the motions*. So..."

Molly slammed the box down. "What did you just say?" Her eyes were slits and Olivia could practically feel the earth move under her feet.

"I was actually just about to leave," Olivia said as she twisted around the counter to grab her purse. She needed to get out of there before the entire condo froze over.

"Don't forget your shoes, Olivia," Molly called to her, without taking her eyes off Ben. She pointed to the brown booties strewn across the living room floor.

Like a child, Olivia obeyed and rushed to shove them on her feet.

"You don't have to leave, Olivia," Ben said. His voice sounded sincere but he looked angry.

"It was nice seeing you, Molly," Olivia said as headed for the door. "And Ben, I'll be sure to contact you when I have a list of places for you and Pete to see." She watched his face fall before swiftly shutting the door.

As she made her way to the elevators, she could hear the faint sound of Molly yelling: *I held you back? That's your excuse? Unbelievable!*

Olivia's face burned with embarrassment. She punched the elevator button several times desperate to get some distance from her humiliation. It all made sense last night. *Yeah, let's give in to our feelings.*

Who cares that you just broke up with your girlfriend? Not thinking was turning out to be a terrible idea.

✳ ✳ ✳

"You did *what?*"

Amanda shot out of her downward dog faster than Olivia could register. Their yoga class was about to begin and Olivia figured she would be able to relax more if she got everything that happened with Ben off her chest.

"Hallelujah! There is a God!"

"Hold on. You haven't heard the worst of it." Olivia sat up and leaned back on her hands. "Molly showed up at Ben's condo this morning. She still hasn't moved out of his condo yet."

"No! You're kidding!" Amanda said dramatically as she folded her legs into a pretzel. "Your life is like a soap opera."

"I don't know how I should take that," Olivia mumbled as she buried her face in her hands.

"What are you going to do?"

"I don't know. But based on the way they were fighting this morning, they still have a lot to work out. He's called but I haven't answered."

"Don't avoid him, Olivia. You don't want to lose a friend after all this."

That was exactly what Olivia was afraid of and she should have considered the risk before jumping into bed with him. She couldn't imagine a life without Ben. Her mind started spinning with "what ifs" and she desperately wanted it all to stop.

"I know that look." Amanda folded her arms across her chest. "You're panicking. You want to run."

"You don't know anything." Olivia hated that she was right.

"Do you want my opinion?"

"No."

Amanda ignored her and continued anyway. "You're right, the timing is off. But I think you'll regret it if you don't give it another shot."

"This isn't how normal, stable relationships start, Amanda."

"Yeah, maybe you're right," she said as she played with a loose string on her leggings. "But do you want to be right or do you want to be happy?"

Can't I be both? Olivia thought.

Their yoga instructor entered the room, calling for silence. Olivia turned her body forward and sat cross-legged with her back straight as the soothing sound of crashing waves filled the room. She closed her eyes and tried to forget everything, even if it was just for a little while.

CHAPTER NINE
Something New

By Monday, Olivia still hadn't worked up the nerve to call Ben back. It was the first time that she actually didn't want to talk to him. At least right now she had an excuse. Burdi had talked her and Amanda into going dress shopping for the holiday party and Olivia had just squeezed herself into a ruched, knee-length dress and modeled it in front of a three-panel mirror. It was a beautiful tight iridescent rose gold dress, perfect for a New Year's Eve party. Depending on which angle the light hit it, the dress produced a stunning sheen in an array of colors.

"I love it," Burdi said with the smile of a proud mother.

"Yeah, me too," Amanda said unconvincingly. She stood off to the side in a black satin cocktail dress, looking like she was about to faint from embarrassment. Burdi had forced Amanda into a padded pushup bra. Normally a small B, Amanda kept trying to smash her breasts down to make them look more natural.

"Amanda, stop fussing. You'll thank me later." Burdi dragged out her sentences dramatically as if she were speaking to a child.

"I look like an idiot," Amanda whispered to Olivia. Although, it was clear Burdi overheard from the eye roll she gave the back of Amanda's head.

"Okay, I think found it," Natalie announced as she rushed into the dressing room. She'd been at Burdi's beck and call since they'd arrived at the dress boutique. First, it was to get coffee. Then, it was to take pictures of every dress they tried on. And just a moment ago Burdi sent her to find a hair brooch that probably didn't even exist.

"Ah, that's it. Well done, Natalie." Burdi held it up to the light and admired the glint it produced.

Natalie sighed and plopped into a velvet Victorian chair.

"Could you have Elizabeth put this on hold at the front?" Burdi asked just as Natalie had gotten comfortable.

"I can do it," Olivia said. "I think I'm going to go with this one anyway." She could tell Natalie needed a break and was more than happy to move around. Natalie mouthed a grateful "thank you" to her as she stepped off the pedestal.

"You're up, Pamela." Olivia slapped Amanda's back and walked out of the fitting room into the main room of the boutique.

As she made her way to the front, women surrounded her, trying on dresses and digging through sale racks. She passed a wedding section filled with dramatic gowns, sparkling jewelry, and lacey lingerie. Veils hung carefully from a giant hat rack and white shoes were arranged neatly in a corner.

Olivia couldn't believe how many little things went into dressing a bride, let alone an entire wedding. It seemed excessive to her. She'd always lived simply, only buying what she needed. Not only did her medical bills make for a tight budget but she never really saw the point of being the most decorated person in the cemetery.

When she was seven, her dad caught her writing her will. It was a few months after her mother passed away. She figured it was necessary since she had so many stuffed animals and wanted to make sure they were taken care of when she was gone. "You don't need to do this!" he shouted as he held up the crinkled piece of lined paper. Olivia had never seen her father so upset. He rarely raised his voice. But the anger drained from his face as quickly as it had come and they never spoke about it again.

Behind the checkout counter at the front of the shop, Olivia found a gorgeous, white-haired woman wearing a smart blue suit and pearls.

"Do you mind putting this on hold for Burdi?" She handed over the brooch.

"Of course." Elizabeth took it from her, checked the back for the style number, and started plugging the information into a flat-screen computer. "Although, knowing Burdi, I'm sure she'll change her mind." She looked up at Olivia and wrinkled her nose playfully.

"It seems busy for a Monday. Is this normal?"

"Just about."

Olivia spun around taking in the activity of boutique once more. Most of the women were searching for a wedding dress. A woman to her left clapped, knowing that she had found the right one, while another was being measured and pinned by a seamstress.

Will I ever have this experience? she wondered. Her lungs suddenly felt tighter, giving her the answer. It seemed that, now, moments she would never have noticed before would taunt her. As if to say: *Sorry, not in your lifetime.*

Elizabeth continued, not noticing the dark cloud that had moved in over Olivia. "Honey, if there's one thing I know it's that love will always find a way, even on a Monday." She smiled as she carefully tucked the brooch into a safe place behind the counter. "And that is what keeps me in business."

After ringing up her dress, Olivia made her way back to the dressing room. She felt heavy like she was walking through water. Everything around her seemed to be moving in slow motion.

She passed a jewelry display case where a sparkling bracelet caught her eye. White gold had been pressed and shaped into tiny little flowers that linked together to form a chain. The flowers were simple: six flat leaves and a diamond center. They reminded her of dogwood flowers.

Her hand reached up to the glass door and she knew as soon as she touched it she would have to have it. The case opened and she carefully slipped the bracelet off of its holder. It shone perfectly in her hand and she smiled as she crossed back over to the checkout counter. It might have been a little out of character, but it was something new.

✳ ✳ ✳

Olivia sifted through her mail as she climbed the flight of stairs to her apartment. When she looked up, there he was: arms folded and leaning against her door. She should be surprised to see Ben there, but she wasn't. The two stood in the hallway, staring at each other like two cowboys about to duel. But she didn't want to be the first one to speak.

"I figured showing up unannounced was the only way I was going to be able to talk to you."

"Ben—"

"We have sex and then I don't hear from you. What am I supposed to think?"

"I know. I'm sorry." But Olivia stopped and shook her head. "Wait a minute. I'm not supposed to feel bad. You're supposed to feel bad!"

She unlocked her apartment door and pushed him inside. "You know exactly why I haven't called you back." She threw her keys on the counter and took a deep breath. "Or did you forget the lovely encounter we had with your ex-girlfriend?"

"Oli—"

"—No, I'm not done." Olivia took a deep breath as she started to feel a strain in her lungs. "You tell me that you don't regret anything but then the minute you see Molly its: *Olivia is just helping me find a space for my restaurant.* I was humiliated."

"You're right. I'm sorry." He pinched the bridge of his nose. "I just... didn't want it to look like I was rubbing it in her face. It didn't seem like the right time to tell her."

"There's that timing issue again," Olivia mumbled. She crossed her arms over her chest. His logic made some sense but she didn't want to admit it. She took slow, deep breaths to calm down but each one stung.

"I'm sorry," he said again and took a cautious step closer, testing the waters.

Olivia's arms, however, stayed tightly crossed like a protective barrier. "Is it over?" she asked. "I need to hear you say—"

Before she could finish, Olivia was interrupted by a strong cough. And almost immediately, a sharp pain erupted from her right side and she doubled over from the pain. She clutched her chest and felt her legs buckle beneath her.

"Olivia?" Ben crouched down by her side.

She didn't answer him. She couldn't answer him. All she could do was look up at him, her eyes begging for the pain to stop.

"I'm calling for help." Ben pulled out his phone and started rattling off Olivia's condition and address to the dispatcher on the other end.

Olivia knew this pain. She'd had it before. Every inhale and exhale felt like a knife was digging into her side. She didn't want to breathe but she had to keep trying.

Ben was speaking to her but she couldn't focus. She just wanted to lie down and wait for the pain to stop. Her heart raced and she felt dizzy. Her head wobbled forward and her vision blurred. The last thing she saw was her arm hitting the floor, her new bracelet sparkling in the light of a beautiful sunset that streamed through her living room window.

CHAPTER TEN
A Full Life

It was dark and windy. Olivia knelt before a candle, desperately trying to light it but every strike of her match seemed useless. She created a protective dome around the wick with her body. Finally, the match lit! Slowly, she moved the delicate flame toward the wick as the wind whipped around her. It fluttered violently but didn't go out. Just a little closer... puff! A curling line of smoke drifted up from the match. As the smell of sulfur hit her nostrils, a slow clock tick started to pulse in her ears: tick, tick, tick... It echoed louder: tick, tick, tick...

A faint, rhythmic beeping overlapped the ticking. As she slowly became conscious, she could hear hushed voices nearby.

"Why did she faint?"

"It was most likely a combination of a few things: the pain from the pneumothorax, the anxiety of the experience. She was also very dehydrated."

Her lung collapsed. Olivia knew she recognized the pain. She slowly moved her fingers and toes. She could feel a tube inserted into the right side of her chest, a few inches below the base of her armpit. *Thank God I was unconscious for that*, she thought. The tube would help remove air from the collapsed portion of her lung but it was easily one of the most painful procedures Olivia ever had to endure—one that she'd gone through three times now.

She carefully opened her eyes to the harsh fluorescent lights shining above her. Grey ceiling tiles came into focus, then a window to her left and a door to the right. Her father stood at the foot of her bed with Dr. Katz, speaking softly. They didn't see her stir so she took the opportunity to eavesdrop.

"Her right lung has become extremely weak in a very short amount of time. She's in danger of more complications than a collapsed lung: infections, respiratory failure—"

"It's time for a transplant. She told me." Her father ran his fingers through his hair. "How soon does she need to make a decision?"

"As soon as possible." Dr. Katz paused before continuing. "We need to get the surgery done within the next 12 to 18 months or else I fear she'll be too sick to operate on."

Olivia gasped. Dr. Katz and her father turned at the sound but she managed to convince them she was just waking up. Her father rushed to her side and took her hand. His face was calm and reassuring as if the previous conversation with Dr. Katz never happened.

"Hi, baby. How are you feeling?"

"A little winded," she said and cracked a hesitant smile. "What time is it?"

"Just before 10:00 a.m. You slept through the night," Dr. Katz said as he picked up her chart and jotted something down.

She touched her naked wrist. "Where's my bracelet?"

"I've kept it safe," her father replied and pulled out the sparkling chain from his pocket. "Dogwood flowers?" He fixed it to her wrist and she felt relief almost immediately as if she'd been injected with a powerful muscle relaxer.

"I'm sure you're hungry, Olivia. I'll have a nurse bring you something," Dr. Katz said. He nodded in her father's direction before disappearing through the door.

"You're thinking about it, aren't you, Olivia?" her father asked without looking her in the eye.

"Yes," she lied.

"Pray. The answer will come," he answered without hesitation.

It was his solution for just about everything. Olivia differed but bit her tongue. It was not the time or place to have an existential argument with her father.

"I'm sorry to do this to you when you've just woken up but I have to get going. I have AP History in thirty minutes," he said before leaning down and kissing her cheek.

"It's okay. I'll be fine," she said but wasn't sure if she really believed it.

"You will. I know it," He turned and nearly slammed into Ben who came rushing through the door that very moment.

"Olivia, you're awake," he said breathlessly. "Sorry, Jack."

"I'll just leave you two... yeah..." her father trailed off as he grabbed his jacket and awkwardly backed out of the room.

"How are you feeling?" Ben asked.

"Okay, I guess," she said with a shrug.

"I'm so sorry, Olivia. For everything."

"You never answered me."

Ben tilted his head and furrowed his brow.

"Is it over between you and Molly?"

He smiled. "It's over between me and Molly. I promise."

A sweet doughy smell permeated the air and woke up Olivia's senses. She looked down and saw a brown bag in Ben's hand.

"Do I smell—"

"Homemade beignets?" He lifted the bag level to his face.

"You're really good at apologies." She snatched the bag from him and started tearing into them.

"Hey! Save some for me!"

"I thought you made these for me?" she asked through a mouthful of fried dough.

"I'm not *that* good at apologies!"

They started wrestling over the bag. Before long, they were in a powdered sugar fight. One of Olivia's sugar assaults left a stripe of white across Ben's hair. She stopped, amazed as if she was seeing into the future—a future she so desperately wanted to be a part of. Ben took her distraction as an opportunity to lean in and trail kisses down her sugar-covered cheeks and nose. She leaned into it, savoring the warmth that spread through her.

Olivia took his face in her hands. "I'm sorry too. I shouldn't have avoided you. Can we call it square?"

"Square," he agreed.

"I'm not very good at this whole relationship thing."

"Neither am I." He smiled and gently kissed her lips. "But I think we can figure it out together."

✳ ✳ ✳

Olivia sat up in bed and watched the sunset through her hospital room window. The colors warmed the grey room and the bouquet of pink roses from Burdi produced a sweet, fresh scent. She twirled her dogwood bracelet around her wrist, watching it leave tiny flecks of light across her skin.

She was exhausted but wanted to keep herself up so she could get back to a regular sleep schedule. Ben, however, was slumped in a chair in the corner of the room, snoring loudly. Amanda, Pete, and Burdi all stopped in to visit but Ben never left. She smiled and watched his chest rise and fall, his face calm and relaxed.

Olivia will be discharged tomorrow morning but she was tempted to sneak out tonight. Her oxygen nose line felt like it was strangling her. She was anxious and uncomfortable—a strange feeling for such a familiar place.

A stack of pamphlets sat on her lap. She was hoping that reading through the lung transplant information one more time would help her decide but she was still torn. A lung transplant wasn't a solution. It was just a way to give her more time. Not only would she have to wait and hope for a proper donor, but she'd also have to live through a complicated procedure. If she did survive the surgery, her body could reject the new lung at any time. And if it didn't, only about half of Cystic Fibrosis patients survive more than five years post-transplant.

What kind of a life would it be with intense surgeries, long hospital stays, and risks of complications? She could only hold on to the hope that she would get more time. But to do what? She didn't have any kids. She wasn't married. She lived with her three-legged cat and frequently binge-watched The Golden Girls.

Olivia looked up at the ceiling. *What do I do? Hello? Anyone there?* She shook her head. She wasn't cut out for this praying stuff.

She didn't want to be another tragic story that people told each other over sips of coffee but she was beginning to think that will be her destiny. She'd be the subject of whispers and gossip just like her mother was.

Olivia didn't have a perfect life nor had she been a perfect person. Facing mortality had forced her to look at her life in a much more vulnerable light: failures screamed at her and mistakes she couldn't undo haunted her. She couldn't change her past but she did have control of her future. And she refused to be miserable.

Olivia's head bobbed to the side. The urge to sleep was officially winning. She let her head fall back on her pillow and closed her eyes.

Olivia sat on the floor in front of a coffee table wrapped in a blanket. Her chest was tight and her voice was raspy. She'd been battling pneumonia for over two months. A few minutes ago, her mother went into the kitchen to get some water but Olivia could hear her quietly crying through the wall.

Earlier her mother had gotten a phone call, probably from one of Olivia's doctors. They had been concerned with how long it was taking her to fight off the infection.

Olivia slid a puzzle piece back-and-forth on the table with her pointer finger. "Mommy?" she called, hoping she could get her distracted again.

"On my way!" her mother said as cheerfully, but her voice cracked. She rushed into the room and dropped down to her knees across from Olivia. Her eyes had lost their sparkle and her skin was paper white. Olivia tried not to stare.

"This puzzle is hard," Olivia said, wrinkling her nose.

"Lots of things are hard, sweetie," her mother muttered as she tried to fit two edge pieces together. When they didn't fit, she pushed the pieces away and buried her head in her hands.

"Mommy, do you want to do something else?"

"No, that's okay," she said as she lifted her head and brushed tears from her cheeks.

"I'm sorry, Mommy."

"You have nothing to be sorry about, sweetie. I'm just having a bad day."

"Is it because I'm sick?"

She looked at Olivia, surprised. "No, of course not! It's just a cold. There's nothing to worry about." She went back to working on the puzzle.

"But it's not a cold. I have 65 roses."

She looked up at Olivia, her eyes wide. "You will get better, Olivia."

"But I won't. Not really," she argued.

"Enough!"

Olivia jumped and tears quickly filled her eyes.

"I'm so sorry, sweetie. I didn't mean to yell," she said gently.

Olivia didn't respond. She just sat there, quivering.

"I think it's time for your physiotherapy. Why don't you go upstairs and I'll meet you in your room with your nebulizer?" Her mother reached across the table and squeezed her hand.

Without a word, Olivia slowly climbed the stairs. But instead of going to her room, she stopped at the top, turned, and sat with her hands over her eyes and cried into them.

Just then, her father came in through the back door. Olivia held her breath to quiet her crying. She didn't want him to know that she was within earshot.

"Jane, what's wrong? Where's Olivia?"

"She's upstairs," her mother answered with a shaking voice.

Her father disappeared behind the staircase. Olivia could hear them speaking but it sounded like she had earmuffs on.

"The hospital called," Her mother continued. "She's not getting better so they want to pump her with more medication and do more tests. Like she's some kind of lab rat."

"We have to trust them, Jane. They're doing everything they can to get her better."

"But she won't get better! That's the problem!"

"Jane—"

"Every time we think we have it under control something else pops up. I don't want to send her to the hospital anymore! Why can't I just give her chicken noodle soup like every other mother?"

"I know. I wish the same things you do, believe me. Please, sit down. Let's talk—"

"No, I need to go for a drive. I need to clear my head."

Olivia heard the jingle of keys.

"Jane, please stop. You're upset. You shouldn't drive right now."

Her mother appeared from behind the stairs. She glanced up and right into Olivia's eyes. "I love you," she breathed. The sound barely reached Olivia's ears. Then, she turned, opened the door, and disappeared into the night.

Olivia jolted awake. Tears stained her cheeks and beads of sweat lined her brow. She tried to slow her breathing but her heart was beating out of her chest. If only she could calm herself. If only she could say: It was just a dream.

CHAPTER ELEVEN
Will B. Under

"Are we there yet?" Olivia shouted above Ben and Pete singing along with the radio. "I thought you said the party was on U Street?"

Olivia sat in the back seat of Pete's car, dressed as Poison Ivy, blindfolded. Today was her birthday. It was also Halloween.

"We're pulling up now!" Amanda yelled above the music. She sounded like an exasperated mother. The car stopped and the music died along with it.

Pete groaned. "Come on, Amanda. Couldn't you let the song finish? Party pooper."

"Can I take this blindfold off now?" Olivia asked.

"Stop asking questions and just go with it," Ben whispered in her ear then kissed her cheek.

Olivia blushed. Thankfully the blindfold was covering half of her face.   She felt a cold gust of air as she was pulled out of the car by her wrist. She followed her escort, slow and awkward, taking cautious blind steps.

"Come on, Olivia, trust us," Pete said through laughter. Apparently, her movements were hilarious.

"Does someone have my oxygen tank?" She frowned thinking of the bulky backpack. Before, she only wore her oxygen line at night. Now, she had to lug a portable one around everywhere she went.

"I've got it!" Amanda called. She slipped the backpack over Olivia's shoulders.

"Do you think I can make this part of my costume?" she asked.

"Did Poison Ivy ever have a jetpack?"

"Definitely not," Pete replied.

"Steps!" Ben shouted. Olivia's heels thumped as she made her way up, Pete and Ben supporting her on either side.

"Ready?" Ben said in her right ear.

"For what?" she asked.

Before she got an answer, the blindfold fell from her face. It took a moment for her eyes to re-adjust but she soon saw that she was facing the back door of her father's house.

"What's going on? I thought we were going to a party?"

"We are!" Amanda said with excitement pinching her face and she pushed open the door.

"SURPRISE!!"

A wave of voices and faces hit her like a truck. Her father, cousins, aunts, uncles, old college friends and co-workers were there—all in an array of crazy costumes. She was immediately overwhelmed.

"H-Hi?" Olivia sputtered, not knowing what to say and laughter rolled through her audience.

"Happy Birthday, Honey." Her father stepped forward dressed as Abraham Lincoln. "Let's have some fun!"

Olivia's childhood home had been completely transformed. Webs stretched across pictures and windows, pumpkins and black candles lined every table, and skeletons hung like limp puppets against the walls.

She spotted Burdi, dressed as Cruella Deville, talking with her father next to a giant punch bowl filled with a bright green liquid.

"Olivia, honey, you never told me your father was so charming." Burdi brushed her hand across her father's shoulder and her father chuckled, clearly enjoying the attention. Olivia suddenly got the urge to crawl into a nearby closet.

"Burdi, is Bruce here? I'd love to say hi." She secretly hoped that mentioning Burdi's boyfriend would remind her to keep a safe distance from her father.

"Yeah, he's off somewhere." She waved her hand in the air as if she was fighting off a pesky fly. "Here..." she poured some of the bright green mixture into a glass. "Have an apple martini. Drink it down and loosen it up!" She kissed her glass to Olivia's then dumped the remaining contents down her throat. "I guess my hands are free for some dancing. Jack, would you like to join me?"

Her father's face lit up. "I'd love to."

Olivia watched them head to the dance floor, which was essentially the living room rug, and shook her head.

"Ready for your present?"

Olivia turned around to see Amanda holding a huge gift bag up to her face. She wore a simple white shirt that said "Go Ceiling" and held a set of pompoms.

Olivia smiled and took the present from her. "What are you supposed to be anyway?"

"I'm a ceiling fan! Get it?" She waved her pompoms around.

Olivia stared at her blankly.

"Well you all said I couldn't be a cat again," she argued.

Olivia snorted and leaned over to drop her martini glass off on the counter. As she did, she spotted Amanda's boyfriend standing a few feet away, not in costume.

"Oh! Hey, Eric. I didn't see you there."

Eric simply lifted his beer to her in acknowledgment.

"Geez, what's his problem?" Olivia asked in a hushed tone.

"Don't worry about him. He's just being an extra asshole today," she whispered back.

Olivia opened her mouth to press her for more details but stopped herself. It wasn't worth it. "Well, anyway, you really didn't have to get me anything. You already did all of this." She gestured to the activity around her.

"This," Amanda said, mimicking her gesture, "was all Ben and your dad." She tilted her head backward and added loudly in Eric's direction: "Ben's an amazing boyfriend."

Eric grumbled and walked away.

Before Olivia could ask, Amanda stopped her. "Open it!"

"Okay, okay." Olivia's lips tilted into a crooked smile as she dug into the gift bag. A large emerald purse waited for her at the bottom.

"Now you don't have to carry around that hideous backpack," Amanda said. "Your portable tank should fit perfectly in this bad boy."

Olivia held the purse up to the light reverently. "It's beautiful! Thank you." Olivia pulled her in for a hug.

"Glad you like it. Here," she took the bag from her, "I'll take this to the gift table. Go have some fun!" She bumped Olivia with her hip before disappearing into the crowd.

Olivia looked back at the dance floor. Burdi was now arguing with

Bruce while her father danced nearby, unfazed by the fighting couple next to him. Olivia laughed and shook her head. The people in her life were ridiculous.

She finished her martini, then squeezed past the "Fear Pong" table to find Ben. She wandered through the small rooms, even smaller now with so many people crammed inside, and tried to say "hello" and "thank you for coming" to everyone she passed. But soon she felt as though she was on autopilot. Every person she passed was part of her. How would she say goodbye when the time came?

On her way into the dining room, she tripped over a foam headstone. As she bent down to put it back into place, she read its face: "Will B. Under." Olivia stopped and stared for long ticking seconds. She felt the apple martini in the back of her throat. Desperate for air, she pulled open the sliding glass doors behind her and burst through the threshold like a born-again Christian.

She took a deep breath, welcoming the cold air into her lungs as a way to sober her emotions. But it only brought temporary relief. Soon the air sucked all the warmth from her body and she hugged her arms around her center to keep warm.

She looked up at the sky. Only a few stars burned bright enough to peak through the bright city lights and dark clouds. "Are you trying to torture me? Is this funny to you?" she yelled.

Her lungs seized up and she delicately coughed to get rid of the discomfort. She held the stitches still on the side of her rib cage as if too much pressure would make them burst open like a balloon.

"Who are you talking to?"

Olivia turned to see Ben staring at her. His face was twisted in amusement.

"No one. I'm fine," she said, anticipating his next question. She looked away and leaned against the deck's cold wooden railing. The floorboards behind her creaked as he took the spot next to her.

"You're a terrible liar."

"I feel like I should go skydiving or ride a bull. Isn't that what dying people are supposed to do?"

"Personally, I've always wanted to own a cow."

"What?" she said with a laugh.

"I could make my own cheese!"

She nudged him playfully and shook her head.

"Do you want to do those things?" he asked, amusement still clinging to his face.

She shrugged. "I haven't exactly lived an impressive life."

"You got me to fall for you. I think that's pretty impressive."

She looked at him sideways. "Smooth."

"Your life isn't over until it's actually over, Olivia. Just keep doing the things you love."

"I'm going to do it... I'm going to get the lung transplant." She didn't know when she decided. Maybe she always knew.

He sighed. "Would it be incredibly selfish of me to say I'm relieved?"

She smiled. "Maybe a little."

He kissed the top of her head. "I want you to fight. I need you to fight."

She wrapped her arm around his bicep and leaned against him. He was warm and strong and she felt like she could melt right into him.

"Do you believe in heaven?"

"I don't think this is the end," he said after a beat.

"Really?"

"Sure. Why not?"

"I don't know. It just... seems a little foolish."

"Maybe, but at least it's comforting."

"I'm terrified of dying, Ben."

He cleared his throat and she realized that this was the first time they'd ever talked about her dying. They always ignored the inevitable, even if it was implied.

"All I know is: whatever happens I'll see you again," he said. "I have to." He wrapped his arms around her.

She desperately wanted him to be right. She'd never wanted anything more in her life.

"Can you stay with me tonight? I don't want to be alone."

"Of course." He leaned down and planted a long kiss on the crown of her head.

"Why aren't we fighting?"

"Should we be?" he asked in amused surprise.

"It seems like every other couple at this party is fighting."

"Don't worry, we have plenty of time to fight."

Olivia smiled and closed her eyes, trying to memorize this moment. She didn't want to forget this feeling: the strength of Ben's arms wrapped around her, protecting her. If only he could protect her from everything.

CHAPTER TWELVE
Ginger Rogers

A single orange rose greeted Olivia outside her apartment door with a note attached:

You owe me a date.
7:00 – Wear your dancing shoes.

She smiled as she picked up the flower and pushed through the rusted door of her apartment. Thankfully, nothing had changed between her and Ben. It felt like it always had, only more comfortable. As if surrendering to their feelings made all the pieces of a puzzle fall into place.

Minkus met her at the door and she bent down to scratch the top of his head. With a tight breath, she decided to flip on her oxygen tank. She wrapped the tubes around her ears, matching the nasal passages up to her nostrils. The cool air hit the back of her nose and traveled down her throat. She closed her eyes and followed the air's path as she inhaled.

With the oxygen line trailing behind her, she dropped the rose into a mason jar and filled it halfway with cool tap water. The jar sat alone on her bare kitchen counter. She watched it for a moment, as light from the setting sun outside her living room window plunged through the water and glass, producing soft blobs of light. She leaned her chin onto her hands and stared at the rose's delicate orange petals.

She worried going out tonight would feel like celebrating and she definitely didn't feel like celebrating. She'd officially given Dr. Katz the "OK" to proceed with the transplant process. Over the next few weeks, she would have to undergo a series of chest x-rays, blood tests, CT scans, breathing and exercise tests to determine if she was healthy enough. If she passed every single one, only then would her name be submitted for a transplant. Just the thought of it all made her dizzy with exhaustion.

A faint meow made its way up to her from the floor. She looked down to see Minkus sitting poised and wide-eyed below. "I guess you're hungry, huh?" she said and pushed off from the counter.

As she set his food down on the floor, the dark emptiness of her apartment caught her attention. The sun had almost finished its descent behind the city skyline and a fan of shadows striped across the floor. The overwhelming quiet rang in her ears. She had a long, hard road ahead of her. She knew she had people in her life who would help her through it but, for some reason, the thought didn't comfort her. She would still have to fight all on her own.

It wasn't the first time Cystic Fibrosis managed to make her feel isolated and alone. A hollow, weak feeling built inside her but she pushed it away. *I refuse to be miserable... I refuse to be miserable...* she repeated the mantra in her head, hoping it would fill the void growing in her stomach. *I refuse to be miserable... I refuse to be miserable...*

The glowing clock above the oven caught her eye: 5:07. She needed to fit in some physiotherapy before her date with Ben. But she couldn't find the energy through her hopelessness to move. Her feet stayed planted as if her shoes were made of lead.

But then she remembered what Ben had said on her birthday: *Your life isn't over until it's actually over.* She refused to wallow. Instead, she was going to celebrate.

✳ ✳ ✳

When Ben arrived, Olivia was running around her apartment with one shoe on. "I'll be right there!" she yelled from inside her closet. "I just have to find my other shoe!" Tossing a box of sweaters to the side, she finally found it flattened underneath. "Gotcha," she mumbled and hopped out of the closet.

Across the room, Ben squinted down at an unfinished puzzle scattered across an old card table. Just the sight of him made her cheeks burn and her knees go weak.

"Remind me again why you love puzzles so much?" he asked as he examined a piece.

"Well, my mom loved them. So, I think that's part of it…" Olivia said as she slid her arms into a brown leather jacket. "I guess I love that, at first, you have this crazy mess in front of you and nothing really makes sense. But then it slowly starts to take shape and you start working even faster, when finally… you're done. And you can look back at this perfect image that actually does make sense."

He laughed. "Are you saying there's existential beauty in a jigsaw puzzle?"

"Yes, I am," she deadpanned.

Ben smiled then looked down at her feet. "Those are your dancing shoes?"

She followed his gaze to her navy blue flats. "They are if you don't want to carry me by the end of the night."

"I have to say, I'm a little disappointed. I would have paid big money to see you dance in heels."

"Sorry to disappoint." She picked up her purse. "Where are you taking me anyway?"

"Don't worry. You'll love it." A wicked smile played on his lips.

"I don't like that look."

Olivia and Ben walked arm-and-arm down an uneven brick sidewalk in Old Town. When they reached the end of the block where a corner store and a dive bar met, Ben led her across the street to an alley. Olivia's eyes followed the crumbling brick, deeper into the dark side street ahead. A steep staircase with an iron railing disappeared beneath the asphalt below a marquee that read: "Ruby's Release: Dance Studio."

The studio was bright and welcoming despite the fact that it lived underground. They filed into a large room with floor-to-ceiling mirrors covering three of the four walls. Couples ranging from teenagers to senior citizens trickled in, gradually filling up the room.

Olivia's lungs had been easily fatigued over past few weeks and she worried dancing would be too much for her. She got winded just talking for long periods of time. But she didn't want to spoil Ben's plans so she kept her concerns to herself.

"You do remember that we're both horrible dancers, right?" she asked as she leaned her back against a balance bar and dug through her purse.

"That's exactly why we need the class."

"We could just go to the bar next door. We're better at drinking." She pulled out her inhaler casually, as if it was a piece of gum, and began taking deep grateful breaths.

"Stop ruining the romance. You're not talking me out of this one."

I'm ruining the romance because I don't want to dance not because of my nerdy inhaler? She dropped the inhaler back in her purse, pushed off from the bar, and slid her hands up Ben's chest. "Or we could just go back to my place…" She started to nibble a trail up his neck.

Ben sucked in a breath. "Oh…"

"Ben! You made it!" They broke from their embrace to see a beautiful dark-haired woman barreling toward them. "How the hell are ya?"

"Sofia! It's great to see you."

The woman squealed and pulled Ben in for a tight hug. Olivia suddenly had the urge to take off her earrings.

"Olivia, I don't know if you remember but Sofia was the manager at Henry's Diner while I worked there," Ben said.

Relief washed over Olivia, melting her stony appearance. She was secretly embarrassed for jumping so quickly to jealousy. While Sofia was a long-legged, voluptuous woman who could steal the heart of any man, she had absolutely no interest in men.

"I remember," Olivia said, shaking her hand.

"Olivia, it's so good to see you. You look great."

Olivia blushed, not immune to Sofia's charm. "Likewise. Are you taking this class too?"

"No, my wife owns the place," she replied proudly. "So, Ben," she said abruptly and slapped him on the shoulder. "Are you here to give me a job at your restaurant or what?" She sent Olivia a playful wink and Olivia's heart fluttered.

"But you have a job," Ben teased.

"Oh, please. A monkey could run this studio. I miss the fast pace of a restaurant!"

"I'll think about it," he said with an unconvincing smile.

"You're cruel."

"Alright, everyone, gather around! We will be starting shortly." A tall, slender woman with a low bun entered the room.

Sofia leaned in toward Ben. "You know I'm the only one you would trust. Call me!" She turned and blew a kiss to the blonde at the front of the room before scooting out the door.

"You're going to hire her, right?"

"Of course."

"Hello, everyone! And welcome!" Ruby put her hands in the air and the chatter in the room subsided. "I'm Ruby and I will be your instructor for the evening. Tonight you will learn the Foxtrot, which reached its peak of popularity in the 1930s. The dance is similar to a waltz, combining short and long steps..."

"I just hope I can actually get this restaurant off the ground," Ben whispered.

Olivia was surprised to hear him admit it. She took his hand. "You'll get it off the ground," she said, looking him in the eye. "But only if you hire Ruby."

"Very funny."

Olivia smiled then turned her attention back to the front of the room. Ruby's partner, who had a bun just like her, appeared by her side. "Now, just so that you all have an idea of where this is going, Hank and I will demonstrate."

Ruby and Hank embraced. Their frames were level with their shoulders and they moved perfectly in unison. Slow – Slow – Quick – Quick. Slow – Slow – Quick – Quick. They turned and stepped in beautiful fluid movements. Slow – Slow – Quick – Quick. Slow – Slow – Quick – Quick. After a few turns, they stopped and bowed. The room erupted in applause.

"Well, come on! Grab your partner and stop looking so terrified." Ruby smiled and nervous laughter radiated over the room. "First, we'll work on your frame. Hank and I will come around to help you."

"Still think this was a good idea?" Olivia asked Ben as she turned to face him.

"Yes," Ben said weakly.

Luckily, the Foxtrot was a relatively tame dance and they stopped often for correction. The only time Olivia did get out of breath is from laughing so hard. They were terrible. They looked like two Muppets trying to fight. But by the end of the lesson, they were able to get a few steps in without tripping over each other.

"We're doing it!"

"I'm just glad I haven't stepped on your feet yet," Ben said, looking down between them.

"Shh! You're going to jinx it."

"We should try a dip."

"No, we shouldn't!"

"I'm the leader, aren't I?"

Ben tipped her backward and Olivia arched her back as much as she could. But her flats couldn't hold the angle and her feet flew out from under her. They both tumbled to the floor. Ben landed on top of her and shook with laughter.

"I told you not to!" Olivia's face flushed as the couples around them turned to stare.

"Hey, isn't this how we met?" Ben's laughter subsided and his eyes fixed on Olivia. He leaned forward and kissed her gently. And soon, everyone else in the room faded away.

CHAPTER THIRTEEN
Thankful

"This is the last option I have for you. So if you don't like it, it's back to the drawing board," she told Ben. The two stood shivering in front of a crumbling twentieth-century brick building on the corner of a busy market street in Northwest D.C.

Olivia had shown Ben six other spaces for his restaurant and at this point, she was mentally and physically exhausted. She'd had pickier clients for sure, but at least they knew exactly what they wanted. Ben, she'd learned, went by the feeling of a place. Whether a space was too pretentious or too bland, Ben "Goldilocks" Luckette always had a reason. "I'll know in my gut when it's right," he promised after the fifth showing. With Thanksgiving only a week away, she was hoping this was lucky number seven.

A cracked sidewalk surrounded the two-story building and the small parking lot in the back was riddled with graffiti. The left side was stained with black soot from a recent fire and one of the front windows was currently being held together with duct tape.

"You *did* say you were okay with a fixer-upper," she said to fill the silence as they walked up to the landing.

"I have a feeling…" Ben said, his eyes bright.

"Wait, really? Let me punch in the code."

Ben's excitement radiated off him and Olivia could feel her body beginning to absorb it. Her hands shook and butterflies bounced around her stomach as she broke open the lockbox.

Olivia pushed the door open and a cloud of dust greeted them. She coughed and wrapped her scarf around her mouth to create a makeshift dust mask.

As they made their way inside and looked around, she started to wonder if "fixer-upper" was putting it too gently. The walls had been stripped down to their studs. Drop cloths covering lumpy mounds hung in the air like ghosts. The floors were only half finished, revealing sandy concrete underneath and an intricate water stain bled across the ceiling. The only object that seemed to be completely intact was a large curving staircase that hid in the shadows against the back wall.

"The previous owner was renovating but went bankrupt before finishing. His plans were to make this a bar so I'm sure we'll find it under one of these cloths." She started to pick up the corner of one but the fabric was sticky and heavy so she decided against it. "There are already appliance hookups in the back for a kitchen. The brick is all original and the foundation looks to be in pretty good shape, but I would recommend calling a—"

"Olivia, shh!" Ben put his finger over her mouth. "Take it in first." He closed his eyes and inhaled.

Olivia smiled behind his finger. "We should probably check for asbestos and mold too," she mumbled.

"I can see it," he said before removing his finger. "Bar area here, booths there, private parties upstairs. We even have room for live music."

She looked around. It would take a lot of work but the space could be beautiful. "It's a great up-and-coming neighborhood and you can't beat the price," she said with a shrug.

"Come on." Ben grabbed her hand and they carefully stepped over loose floorboards and puddles, crunching dirt and debris under their feet. "Have you gotten your test results?" he asked as they toured the would-be kitchen.

"Not yet. I'm sure with Thanksgiving next week they'll be a little delayed."

Ben nodded and they walked toward the curving staircase. It had been a week since Olivia took her first round of tests. She tried to sound hopeful but the tests ahead were looking more and more daunting.

"Do you think these are safe to climb?" A few of the staircase steps lifted and curled at the ends.

"I won't let you fall." Ben threaded his arm through hers and Olivia was immediately warmed by his touch.

At the top of the stairs, they found a door tucked away in a corner. Ben wiggled the knob free to reveal a large room with windows that opened to the back parking lot.

"The listing did mention an office so this must be it," Olivia said as they took a few careful steps inside.

"This is perfect. I could sell my condo to help with the renovations and live here."

Olivia looked around at the dusty room with missing floorboards. "Ben, this isn't livable." And before she knew it, her mouth ran away from her. "If you need to save money you can always live with me." She held her breath. *Did I just ask him to move in with me?*

Ben looked at her sideways and squinted as if he was trying to decide if she really meant it. "I'll keep that in mind," he said with a smile.

Olivia cringed and her cheeks burned.

"Well, you know what I think," he said changing the subject. "What about you?"

"Who cares what I think? It's your restaurant," she replied.

"I do. Your opinion's important to me."

She paused and looked around. "It'll be a lot of work but I think it's perfect. That staircase is breathtaking."

"I agree." His eyes fixed on her and suddenly she wasn't so sure he was talking about the staircase. He took her face in his hands and planted a soft kiss on her lips. She pulled him closer and they made love right there in the unlivable room.

✳ ✳ ✳

It was a cold but sunny Thanksgiving Day. Leaves swirled around Olivia as she placed her right hand on the cold leather ball. She looked up at Amanda who lined up across from her.

"It's on, bitch."

Amanda scrunched her nose. "You scare me."

The "Yams" and the "Turkey Skins" were tied in the last play of the game. Natalie sat bundled up on the sideline with the scoreboard and warm apple cider. She waved to Pete who winked back at her.

"Did you just see that?" Amanda whispered to Olivia. But Olivia didn't have time to respond as Pete set up behind her.

"Alright, Blue Balls 69! Blue Balls 69," he yelled.

Olivia rolled her eyes. Eric and Burdi shifted in response. Sofia squatted down next to Olivia, directly across from her father.

"Watch the left side!" Ben yelled down the line to Bruce and Ruby.

"Ready! Ready! Hut-hut-hike!"

Olivia snapped the ball between her legs and blocked Amanda. To her left, Ruby made a beeline for Pete. "Blitz!" she yelled.

Pete quickly released the ball. It soared over Bruce's head and was caught by Burdi running along the left side of the field. Bruce tried to catch up with her as she ran toward the end zone marked off by water bottles.

"She just... might... go... all... the... way!" Pete yelled in tandem with her run.

Burdi reached the end zone and slammed the ball down in triumph. "Yeah!" she cried as Bruce wrapped Burdi up in a gentle tackle and they fell to the ground laughing.

"Natalie!" Olivia shouted and waved her over.

Natalie jumped up and ran her inhaler over to her. Olivia never had this amount of activity leave her so breathless and, on top of it all, she'd been feeling woozy all day. It was becoming more and more real to her that she needed a transplant.

"Thanks," she said as Natalie handed her the inhaler.

"No problem. I'll grab you some water too," she said before heading back to the sideline.

"Are you okay, honey?" Her father had appeared at her side.

"I'm okay." She took a puff of her inhaler. "Promise."

"Are you okay?" Ben jogged up to her.

"I'm fine," she said curtly. *Do I need to wear a flashing sign on my chest?* she thought.

"I'll go get your water for you." He kissed her temple and ran toward the end zone.

"So, you two are dating, huh?" her father asked as he burned a hole into Ben's back with his eyes.

"I thought you liked Ben."

"Not anymore," he said. "He better be taking care of you." Her father looked down at his feet and started to rock back-and-forth on his heels.

"He is," she assured him. If Ben had promised her anything it was that he would always take care of her. "But he doesn't come close to you," she added and leaned over to kiss him on the cheek.

"Damn right." He wrapped his arm around her shoulders and they walked over to the sideline.

"Do you think Mom would have liked him?" She didn't know why she asked and immediately wished she could take it back. The question made her feel small like she was seven-years-old again.

There was a long, difficult silence before he answered. "Of course." He rubbed his hand over his mouth like he was trying to figure something out. "Of course she would have."

Natalie handed out paper cups filled with steaming apple cider. Everyone gathered around to toast to a year of blessings. But Olivia only feigned gratitude. Her world had flipped upside down and so much uncertainty loomed over her that it seemed impossible to be grateful.

CHAPTER FOURTEEN
Tennis Match

Olivia slumped into an oversized chair in the sunroom of a single-family row house. She'd had this home under her care for almost eight months and finally found a buyer. Looking out at the familiar back patio and lawn, she was almost sad to see it go.

Ticking off a mental "to-do" list, she realized that she could use this time to call the caterer to confirm the menu for the company party. Instead, she pulled out her phone and dialed Amanda's office number. She needed to get to her before Burdi did.

"Amanda speaking," she answered with a sigh.

"You okay?"

"Oh hey, Olivia. What's up?" she asked, ignoring her question.

"Are you free Saturday night?"

"I am now. Eric has to fly out this weekend for a conference. What did you have in mind?"

"Burdi mentioned taking us out—"

"*Hell* no."

"You said you were free."

"Something came up."

"Please?" Olivia begged. "She wants to thank us for helping with the party and I think we deserve a fun night out."

"A night out with my boss is not my idea of fun."

"It won't be anything crazy, just a nice dinner or something."

"I can't believe you're trying to talk me into this."

"Meet me at my place before and I'll get you drunk enough to not care."

"Fine," she conceded. "I'll go."

"Thank you, Amanda. I'll talk to you later."

"Yeah, yeah."

Satisfied, Olivia swung her legs over one arm of the chair and leaned her back against the other. The sun fought its way through the glass windows and warmed patches of her skin. Her eyes became heavy and her breathing slowed.

Just as she was drifting off to sleep, her phone rang, cutting through the quiet. "Ugh, what?" she said as she looked at her phone. She didn't recognize the number but figured she should pick it up in case it was the lab calling with her results.

"This is Olivia," she said groggily.

"Olivia. This is Dr. Katz."

"Oh, hi Dr. Katz…" She sat up immediately. *This can't be good*, she thought. Her body instantly stiffened as she prepared for the worst.

"I wanted to call you about the tests you took the other week."

"Are they that bad?"

"Your results are mostly positive but I wanted to make you aware of something your blood test indicated."

"Okay," she breathed.

"Olivia, you're pregnant."

She almost laughed. There had to be some mistake. She didn't have a regular period let alone an immune system that could sustain a child. "I'm what?" she asked, sure this was Dr. Katz's idea of a sick joke.

"Based on your HCG levels I would estimate you're about eight weeks along, but your gynecologist will be able to verify."

Her throat tightened as bile rose to the surface. She actually felt the blood drain from her face. *Pregnant?* Her hands started to shake. "Are you sure?" she whispered into the phone.

"Olivia, I know this is hard to believe. It's difficult for someone with Cystic Fibrosis to get pregnant but it's still very possible."

Her head was spinning. How did this happen? How was she going to tell Ben? And her father? *Oh God. My father is going to kill Ben*, she thought.

"We're going to need to hit "pause" on the transplant, at least until you decide how you'd like to move forward," Dr. Katz said.

The transplant. She'd been so focused on the news that she completely forgot about the transplant. Her mind was in a blank panic.

When she didn't respond Dr. Katz continued. "I'm going to be

71

honest with you: most women with Cystic Fibrosis plan for months, years even, to have children. With your pregnancy being so unexpected, there is a high risk of miscarriage."

"I understand."

She couldn't take any more information. Short, breathy sentences were all she could provide without vomiting all over the model furniture. She slid onto the floor and folded her knees into her chest.

"Olivia, whatever you decide to do, just know that I will support you."

Whatever I decide to do? What exactly is there to do? It took her a moment, but soon she understood and an intense wave of nausea crashed over her.

"I understand. Thank you, Dr. Katz."

She hung up the phone just as a gluey nausea bubbled in her stomach. She couldn't hold it back any longer. She was going to be sick.

Olivia ran outside to the backyard, fell to her knees, and threw up in a melting pile of snow. She hugged her center as she trembled and cried. She took deep, slow breaths to calm herself while face down in the snow.

After a while, she straightened her stiff legs to stand. The bottoms of her feet prickled and her whole body quivered from the cold. A gust of wind blew past, lifting snow into the air and burning her skin.

Fury began to swell inside her. *How could this happen? How could I be so stupid?* she thought. Angry tears built in her eyes and her hands tightened into fists. Desperate to release the crippling anger that boiled inside her, she picked up a small potted planter and chucked it across the lawn with a grunt. The clay pot shattered as soon as it hit the ground.

Her anger faded and was immediately replaced by an overwhelming sadness. Pressure built behind her eyes and she wrapped her arms around her center in an attempt to hold herself together.

Her world felt so out of balance. Most women would be thrilled to get this kind of news. Instead, she was standing in her own vomit, terrified and angry. She unwrapped her arms and slid her hands to her stomach. *What do I do now?*

CHAPTER FIFTEEN
Buddha Reincarnated

A glass of red wine sat on Olivia's coffee table, taunting her. *If you take a sip, you've made up your mind*, it said. She reached for the glass then pulled her hand back. The routine went on for hours. She didn't get up to turn on the lights when the sun disappeared behind the city skyline.

Eight weeks. Her gynecologist confirmed it. She took a deep breath and her chest burned down the center. *What do I do?*

The answer seemed obvious. She would have a better chance of living if she weren't pregnant. Or would she? She was at the end of her rope anyway…

The tennis match that went on inside her head was maddening. Every time she thought she'd made up her mind, a little voice in her head would yell: *Stop! You have a chance to have something you never thought possible!*

The one person she needed to talk to was the one person she was most terrified to tell. Would it be a burden or a gift? Would he stay or run? She couldn't avoid him forever nor would she be able to hide such a big secret from him for long.

A faint knock came from her front door. Amanda. Olivia had forgotten she was coming over. She wasn't ready for tonight. She wasn't ready to pretend like everything was fine.

She forced herself off the couch and shook her stiff arms and legs in attempts to bring some life back into them. She'd been a hollow shell for almost three days, avoiding everyone with the excuse that she'd been "busy with work." With her hand on the brass doorknob, she forced a smile and opened the door.

Amanda stood before her with a red, swollen face and tears rolling down her cheeks. "He broke up with me!" she said and charged past Olivia into her apartment. "He broke up with me!" She poked her pointer finger at her chest with enough force to leave a bruise.

Olivia closed the door and mentally sighed with relief. Amanda was so wrapped up in her own problems she probably wouldn't be able to read into hers.

"Why is it so dark in here?"

"I…"

"Can I have this?" she asked and lifted the glass of wine to her lips.

"It's all yours. I didn't even take a sip," Olivia said fruitlessly as Amanda started gulping.

Amanda plopped down on the couch dramatically and made a motorboat sound with her lips. Olivia walked over and joined her, trying hard to look like she had her life together.

"What happened?" Olivia asked.

"Well…" Amanda held up a finger as she finished off the rest of the glass. "He told me, with absolutely no remorse, that he's been seeing someone else for six months. Six months!" She poured herself another generous glass. "Can you believe it?"

Her eyes were wide with anticipation and Olivia realized that she was completely serious. It wasn't the time play the I-told-you-so card, so Olivia played along.

"No, I can't."

"Plus, isn't it my job to break up with him when he's the one who screwed up?"

Olivia was at a loss for words. She struggled to gather the love and support she should in her best friend's time of need. "I don't know," was all she could muster.

"I put everything I had into our relationship," Amanda continued, oblivious to Olivia's weak support. "Look at all the time I've wasted on him. Why didn't he just tell me he was unhappy six months ago?" Her voice shook and she sniffed. "I just want someone really cool to hang out with who will love me for the rest of my life. Is that too much to ask?"

Tears began streaming down her face and Olivia wrapped Amanda in her arms. She folded into Olivia's chest like a child. Even though Olivia saw this coming, she hated that this happened to her.

74

"I'm so sorry. You don't deserve this," she said as Amanda started to wail. "If you need a place to stay while this all gets sorted out, you know you can always stay with me." But Olivia immediately felt a twinge of regret as soon as it came out of her mouth. *Why do I keep offering my home to people?* she thought.

Amanda pulled away and looked her, wet-faced and resolute. "No. I'll be damned if he tries to take the apartment too. He's already taken three years of my life."

Olivia smiled. "You deserve better and you're better already without him." She brushed aside a damp chunk of Amanda's hair and smoothed it back into place.

"You're right," Amanda said, with mascara running down her cheeks. "I am."

✵ ✵ ✵

By the time they met Burdi, Amanda was an entire bottle of wine ahead of everyone else. Olivia had tried to hide Amanda's broken heart with makeup and hairspray but the result was only mildly presentable. Her eyes were still puffy, constantly filled with a thin line of tears.

Burdi was suspicious of both Amanda and Olivia as soon as she picked them up. Amanda's drunk was teetering her back-and-forth between soft sobs and giggling hysteria and Olivia couldn't carry a conversation to save her life. She felt queasy as if her own secret was poisoning her from within and needed to be released. At every lull in conversation, it was on the tip of her tongue but never slipped past her lips.

"I thought you said we were just doing dinner?" Amanda shouted over the music as they moved through the crowd.

"Or something!" Olivia corrected.

"You said it would be tame! A nightclub is the opposite of tame!"

"This is what Burdi wanted to treat us to!"

"Oh, well whatever Burdi wants…" Amanda mocked.

They stopped at a secluded booth next to a long silver bar that produced an icy blue glow. A waitress greeted them wearing a black, "single ladies" inspired bodysuit and Burdi took the liberty of ordering everyone tequila shots. Amanda looked green at the idea while Olivia's stomach spiked with anxiety. *You have to tell them*, she thought.

"Alright, what's going on?" Burdi asked as their waitress walked away. "You both have had sticks up your asses since I picked you up."

"Do you think that's why I got dumped?" Amanda asked. "Burdi, am I a perpetual…" she paused and looked around before whispering: "C-U-Next-Tuesday?" But Amanda didn't wait for her to respond. "I am," she nodded, agreeing with herself. "I'm going to work on that." She waved a hand in front of her face to fan away her tears.

"Good God," Burdi mumbled.

"Amanda's breakup with Eric was just bad timing. We really are excited to be here," Olivia assured her.

"I can tell," Burdi said sarcastically as she continued to stare at Amanda.

"Starting now, Amanda and I are committed to having fun!" she declared. It was more of a plea than a promise. Amanda attempted solidarity by forcing her face into delight but she ended up looking more constipated than happy.

"We can go home if you're that miserable," Burdi said.

"No way, we all deserve a night out. Right, Amanda?" Olivia stared at her, begging her to agree.

Amanda nodded weakly.

Their waitress returned with their shots and some limes. She took one look at Amanda and quickly shuffled away.

"What should we toast to?" Olivia asked.

"Well, Burdi's probably on her way to her third marriage and I'm 29 and single again," Amanda giggled without humor.

Olivia's eyes widened. But to her surprise, Burdi reached out and patted Amanda's forearm. Amanda stiffened and looked down at Burdi's hand as if bird poop had just landed there.

"It'll be alright. Men aren't the center of our world, even though they often think they are."

Amanda looked at her in awe, as if she was Buddha reincarnated.

"How about: to new beginnings?" Burdi raised her glass with a smile.

Olivia raised her glass and debated whether or not she could get away with tossing the tequila over her shoulder without anyone noticing. But as their glasses clinked, she couldn't hold it back any longer.

"I'm pregnant," she said.

Amanda, who had already started taking her shot, spit it back into her glass while Burdi slowly lowered her's back down on the table. Olivia, however, stayed frozen with her glass out in front of her. She stared at it, unable to make eye contact with either of them.

Finally, she shrugged and brought the shot toward her lips. But Burdi stopped her. She placed her palm over the opening of Olivia's glass and pushed it back down onto the table.

The club lights started flashing and a deep booming voice came through the speakers. Cheers and applause of unburdened guests surrounded them as the DJ started his set. But their table stayed frozen in time.

"Please don't say anything to anyone," Olivia said. "I haven't figured out how to tell Ben yet." Her eyes shifted back-and-forth between the women facing her. Burdi was the first to speak.

"How far along?"

"Eight weeks," she replied.

Amanda slumped back in her chair and covered her mouth.

"What are you going to do?" Burdi asked softly.

"What do you mean?" Amanda looked at her surprised. "She needs that lung transplant."

"I haven't decided yet," Olivia said.

"Olivia," Amanda said softly, leaning toward her. "You would be risking your life to have this baby."

"I know that it's just..." she shook her head. She didn't know why it was so difficult to put how she felt into words.

But Burdi nodded, showing she understood. "It doesn't have to make sense to anyone but you." She took Olivia's hand and squeezed it.

"Why did I do it?" Olivia said as tears filled her eyes. "I knew it would end in disaster." A single tear escaped and rolled down her cheek. It splashed over the back of Burdi's hand but she didn't let go. "I thought I'd already hit rock bottom but I just keep on tumbling."

"An object in motion stays in motion unless acted upon by an unbalanced force, right?" Burdi said looking around the table for nods of approval. But Amanda and Olivia stared at her blankly so she continued. "Love is that force and you have so much of it surrounding you. Tap into it."

Amanda's mouth fell open. Burdi really was Buddha reincarnated.

"I have an idea," Burdi announced, her eyes bright with mischief. "Excuse me," she stopped a shirtless waiter passing their table. "Is there a place where we can step outside to smoke?"

"Sure, right through those doors," he pointed to a set of double doors a few yards away.

"I'm sorry, but have you been paying attention at all?" Amanda asked, incredulously.

"Let's go," Burdi said, ignoring her.

They followed Burdi out the double doors and onto a concrete patio riddled with cigarette butts. A few yards away was a grimy set of dumpsters overflowing with black trash bags. The freezing air immediately penetrated their clothes and made them shiver.

"Well, this is pleasant," Amanda mumbled.

"I think you both need to let off some steam. So..." Burdi opened her arms wide. "Let it out."

"Huh?" Amanda grunted.

"Scream. Throw punches. Whatever feels right."

"This isn't fight club," Amanda said and quickly pulled Olivia aside. "Okay, she's officially snapped. I'm pretty sure I've seen a horror film that starts out exactly like this. And, spoiler alert: we don't make it out alive," she whispered.

Olivia smiled. Amanda might not like the idea but she was quickly warming to it. She'd been woven too tight for too long. Throughout her life, so many things had made her angry: her Cystic Fibrosis, her mother's death; how nothing ever seemed to go the way she planned. She took a deep breath and screamed as loud as she could.

"Olivia!" Amanda stepped back in shock.

Olivia ignored her and started punching and kicking the black bags around the dumpster. Every expletive she could think of came flying out of her mouth until her voice became raspy.

"Perfect! This is perfect!" Burdi cried with her hands in the air. A sudden streak of lightning would go perfectly with the crazed look in her eyes.

"Olivia, please calm down!" Amanda grabbed her shoulders and pulled her away from the dumpsters.

Olivia's lungs were shot. Her yells only came in short bursts but her hands continued to punch the air. She wanted to drain herself of all the pain and anger she'd been feeling her whole life. She wanted to be numb to it all.

Finally, Amanda gave up and started to yell too. Burdi joined them and the three stood in a circle with their heads tilted to the sky, screaming.

A bouncer suddenly burst through the set of double doors. "What the hell is going on?"

The three women stopped screaming and stared at the bouncer innocently. Burdi stifled a laugh.

"We're done!" Amanda rushed everyone inside past the bouncer and back into the club.

When they reached their table, Olivia was breathless from laughter. "I can't stop! Why can't I stop laughing?" Her voice was hoarse and her chest was tight.

"Life is funny like that, isn't it?" Burdi laughed, wiping a tear from the corner of her eye.

"Just go with it," Amanda said. "Laughing feels so much better than crying."

Olivia smiled, reveling in the warm fatigue in her abdomen. *It really does*, she thought.

CHAPTER SIXTEEN
Cat Chat

Minkus rubbed his face against Olivia's ankles as she leaned over her claw-foot tub to turn on the shower. She was anxious and needed to think so she decided to take a shower because hot showers solve everything.

"How am I supposed to get in with you all over me?" She reached down to rub the back of his neck.

He meowed gratefully.

She stepped into the slick tub and let the hot water wash over her. Closing her eyes, she inhaled deeply through her nose, breathing in the heavy steam.

Her future presented itself once again: she could keep the baby and live another year or two (if she was lucky), or she could get a transplant and live for another five to ten years (if she was lucky). Lately, she'd proven to not be so lucky.

When she opened her eyes, she spotted Minkus, peeking his head through the edge of the shower curtain. A year ago, she found him on the side of the road. A car had hit him. His front right leg was so badly mangled that it had to be amputated. Ever since then, he didn't like leaving her out of his sight.

As she watched Minkus poke his head in and out of the shower curtain, Olivia couldn't help but think that he would need to learn to live without her someday, maybe someday soon.

Panic rose up inside her and pressure built behind her eyes. This time, she didn't fight to hold back her tears. She let them fall. They came so quickly and easily, like a summer storm. A heartbreaking wail escaped her lips and she covered her hand over her mouth. But she continued to force out her tears, hoping to cry enough now so she never had to cry again.

She bent over and curled up into a ball on her shower floor. She was sad, angry, confused, scared, queasy, anxious, and stunned—all at the same time. Her mind was alive and young. She wanted to do so much but her body refused to let her.

She sat up, resting her back against the side of the tub, and let the shower run over her face. The pounding water washed her tears away as if they were never there.

Olivia looked down and saw that her hand had found its way to the base of her stomach. A little piece of her and the person she loved the most in this world was in there. The enormity of what was going on inside of her left her dazed.

It was the only part of her that seemed to be thriving. Her body was incessantly weak and her lungs felt like they were made of chalk, crumbling with every breath. But it surged through her, giving her life. It was the newest part of her, healthy and untouched. She wanted to protect it and keep it that way. She didn't want the world to invade and take away its perfection.

"I'm crazy. I have to be crazy," she said. "Right?" Olivia looked up at her bathroom ceiling. If she was praying it felt strange. She wasn't even sure she believed in God. But soon, her breathing slowed and her tears vanished.

She looked at Minkus, who was still peeking through the curtain. "Am I crazy?"

He meowed his response.

"Yeah," she nodded. "I am crazy."

✳ ✳ ✳

A flurry of activity whizzed around the restaurant as she looked around for Ben. The broken window had been replaced and all the cobwebs cleared. The walls had been patched up and a new, dark maple floor started to make its way across the dining room. Though it was far from complete, the building now looked more like a restaurant than a hobo refuge.

It had been almost a week since Olivia had seen Ben. Luckily, he was so wrapped up in the restaurant remodel that he barely noticed her absence. She was dreading what she had to do but she couldn't put it off any longer. She had to tell him.

"Olivia! Aren't you a sight for sore eyes?" Pete walked over to her with rolls of floor plans in his hands. "Please tell me you'll be hanging around for a bit because I'm sick of being surrounded by all these hairy and sweaty construction workers."

Olivia gave him a small smile. "For a bit. Is Ben around?"

"And here I thought you came to see me," he said with a wink. "He's in the kitchen. I'll go grab him." Pete squeezed her arm before disappearing through a wide doorway in the back.

Olivia stood in the middle of the restaurant, awkwardly wringing her hands and tapping her foot. *Breathe. It'll be okay*, she told herself.

"Hey! I didn't know you were stopping by!"

Ben walked toward her from across the room. He sported a five o'clock shadow and a dusty T-shirt. He couldn't look sexier or happier to see her. She knew he loved her blind but Olivia worried he might regret it soon.

"Is this a bad time?" she asked as he kissed her temple. She leaned into it a little, enjoying his touch. He smelled like wood shavings.

"Not at all. What do you think?" He stretched out his arms to the chaos.

"It looks great."

She must not have said it convincingly because Ben frowned down at her. "You okay?"

She looked up at him. Their eyes connected like two puzzle pieces, a pleasant snap of two fragments coming together that should. The way Ben looked at her was as if he could see all of her, the good and the bad. It left her feeling both vulnerable and euphoric at the same time. She didn't ever want to lose that look and she found herself racking her brain for reasons to keep her secret a little longer.

"Can we talk somewhere private?"

"Yeah, of course," he said after a beat and took her hand.

Olivia followed him up the grand staircase to the office. Her cheeks burned pink as she remembered the last time they were there together. When she stepped inside, she didn't recognize it. The room had been finished and furnished, and now looked like a real office. A desk and two filing cabinets were arranged toward the back of the cream painted room and the couch from Ben's condo faced them.

"This is the only room that's completely finished," Ben said awkwardly. "It's not much but..." He didn't even bother finishing. He looked down at the floor then back up at Olivia.

"I have something I need to tell you," she said turning to face him.

"Okay..." He searched her face.

She let out a heavy breath. "I'm pregnant," she said just above a whisper. Olivia could feel her eyes bulge as she said it as if she was hearing the news for the first time too. "...And I want to keep it," she added quickly before she could stop herself. She held her breath and waited for his response.

Ben couldn't hide the shock that spread across his face. But she was surprised to see a tiny stripe of tears build on the lower rim of his eyes. He gently placed his hands on either side of her face and touched his forehead against hers. They stood with their heads together as long seconds ticked by.

It was not the reaction Olivia had expected. She could feel emotion radiating off him but she didn't know what he was thinking. She needed to keep going, as much as it hurt.

"Ben, I have to give up the transplant... at least for now," she said as the lump in her throat grew bigger. She could feel him shaking as he tried to hold back his tears.

He released her and turned to sit down on the lumpy couch. He rested his face in his hands for a moment then rubbed his eyes like he was trying to wake up from a dream.

"I'll never forgive myself for putting you through this, Olivia. Never. I'm so sorry."

Olivia's heart ached at his reaction, his look of total defeat. She rushed to his side, tears streaming down her face. "You are not to blame for any of this." She took his hands. "We fell in love and our love grew. That's all." She paused and tilted his gaze to hers. "I don't regret any of it. Do you?"

"No," he said. "Just maybe the timing of it." A painful smile peeked at the corners of his lips.

Olivia smiled back.

"What if the baby has...?" He stopped mid-sentence, unable to finish.

"I know. I thought about that too. There's a chance," Olivia admitted weakly. "But look at me. I'm ten years past where doctors thought I'd be when I was first diagnosed. If he or she does have Cystic Fibrosis I know that they'll have a fighting chance."

"I can't live without you, Olivia."

"I can try again for the transplant after the baby," she said. But she knew it was a lie. By that point, it would probably be too late.

Ben looked down at his feet and shook his head as if he knew it too. "What can I do?" he asked.

"Just love me," she said and leaned against his chest. Her head moved up and down with each breath and she tried to match her breathing to his. "And don't ever stop."

"I can do that," he mumbled.

They lay together in silence, melting into one another. There was no beginning or end between them. Their hands clasped tightly together and their legs intertwined. A human infinity symbol.

CHAPTER SEVENTEEN
To the Moon and Back

Olivia stood in front of her bathroom mirror putting on bright red lipstick while her father paced outside the door. She was just as nervous as he was but refused to show it.

"Who is this boy again?"

"Dad, for the millionth time, his name is Rob and I have Physics with him."

"You're putting on too much makeup. You don't need all that."

She rolled her eyes. "It's prom. I'm supposed to put on too much."

"Says who? The same people who say you're supposed to have sex tonight?"

"Dad!"

Olivia felt her cheeks burn with embarrassment. It was times like these that she missed her mother the most. If she were alive, she'd gently slap her father's shoulder and say, "Oh, stop it, Jack!" Then she'd turn to Olivia and whisper, "Don't listen to him." At least, that's how Olivia liked to imagine it.

"Do you have your inhaler? And that pepper spray I gave you?"

"Yes, and yes," she said evenly.

"What time is he supposed to get here?"

"6:00."

"Well, he's late."

"By two minutes!" she closed the cap of her lipstick and walked over to him. "Dad, I love you but you need to relax."

His eyes warmed at the sight of her. "You look stunning, Olivia."

She blushed and looked down at her dark blue satin gown. "Thanks..." she said timidly.

The doorbell rang and Olivia jumped slightly at the sound. "That's probably *him," she said as she moved passed her father.*

"Before you go..." Her father held out his hand to her.

Olivia looked down and saw he was holding a beautiful, sparkling hair comb.

"This was your mother's. I think she would have wanted you to wear it."

"Thank you," she whispered, swallowing back the pressure building behind her eyes. She kissed his cheek before taking the comb from him and gently pressing it to the base of her bun. The blue and white diamonds sparkled against her blond hair.

"I love you to the moon and back," he said.

"To the moon and back," she replied.

✻ ✻ ✻

Olivia rushed around the half-finished dining room lighting candles. The restaurant was the only place she could think of to fit everyone comfortably for a Christmas Eve potluck. She had done her best to put together a homey appearance: a boom box blared Christmas music from the partially stained bar next to a small Christmas tree, white lights stretched from one corner of the room to the next, and Ben had fashioned a long table out of old keg barrels and scrap lumber.

She paused before throwing a white tablecloth over the makeshift table. "Are you sure this is sturdy enough?" she called to him from across the restaurant.

"Nope," Ben said walking toward her with his arms full of wine glasses.

She spread the fabric out and smoothed its surface. "Well, this will be an interesting dinner party then."

"Interesting is one way to put it," he muttered as he set out the glasses.

Olivia looked at him sideways and knew exactly what he meant. They had decided to invite her father over to the restaurant early so they could tell him the news and tension had hung thick in the air ever since.

"You know how we can make this easier?" Ben asked.

"How?" She reached for a pile of napkins.

"If you marry me," he said.

Olivia froze and looked up at him. They stared at each other for a moment. Then, she tossed her head back and laughed. She laughed hard.

"What's so funny?" he asked.

Olivia stopped mid-laugh. "Wait, you're serious?"

"Yes," he insisted as if it should have been obvious. He walked toward her and took her hands. "Will you marry me, Olivia?"

Olivia stared at him in disbelief. "Ben... I'm not going to marry just because I'm pregnant."

"I'm not asking you just because you're pregnant."

She pulled her hands away and placed them on her hips. "Oh, so you were planning on asking me before I got pregnant?"

"Maybe I was!"

"Oh, please. Are you sure it's not just because 'until death do us part' doesn't sound so intimidating anymore?" she blurted out bitterly. "You don't even have a ring!"

The weight of her words fell like a brick between them. Ben's face dropped and regret immediately began bubbling in Olivia's stomach.

"Wow... Is that what you really think?" he said.

Olivia looked down at her feet. "I'm sorry," she said, trying to vacuum up the words that just spilled out. "I didn't mean that. I just don't want to rush anyth—"

"Don't worry about it. I heard you loud and clear." Ben turned and disappeared into the kitchen.

She cursed and slammed down a napkin. The soft thud gave her absolutely no satisfaction. She wanted to get married because it was right for them and their relationship, not because society thought it looked better.

She knew that was not why Ben asked her, though. He loved first and thought second. She was the exact opposite.

The front door to the restaurant swung open and her father walked in with an apple pie in one hand and a bottle of wine in the other. Teddy Roosevelt followed closely on his heels. Ben came running back in from the kitchen and the two of them stood frozen over a pile of napkins.

"Merry Christmas!" Olivia's father exclaimed cheerfully.

"Merry Christmas!" They both answered in unison.

"Here let me help you with that," Ben said as he rushed over to and took the wine from his hands.

"Thank you. I hope this is a good one, Olivia. I know how you love your reds."

"Can I take your jacket?" she asked quickly as she pulled the pie from his other hand.

"Would you like a drink?" Ben asked.

"I'm fine, I'm fine. What's with you two?"

Ben and Olivia looked at each other, then away again.

"Everything's fine, Dad," Olivia said as she rung her hands.

"Well, we do have some… exciting news." Ben said.

Olivia looked at Ben, her eyes wide.

He shrugged as if to say: *Sooner is better than later.*

"About the restaurant?" her father asked, oblivious to their exchange.

"No, not about the restaurant," Olivia said.

"Well, what is it?"

"Dad…" Olivia walked over to him and took his hands. She struggled to speak, her words sticking to the back of her throat. His salt and pepper eyebrows crinkled and wrinkles rippled across his face as he waited.

"I'm… pregnant," she finally said.

Her father's face fell and soon turned whiter than the tablecloth. He took a step back, dropping her hands. He breathed heavily, opening and closing his mouth, unable to find the words.

Ben stepped around Olivia toward her father. "Mr. Hamm—"

Olivia's father suddenly surged forward, grinding his teeth in rage. "You call that exciting news?" He pushed past Olivia and wrapped his hands around Ben's throat. "What the hell did you do?"

"Jesus Christ! Dad!" She tried to get in between them. Ben just stood there limp, taking his punishment.

"What the hell is going on?"

Pete had appeared at the door with a pile of casserole dishes in his hands. He looked confused and stiff, ready to intervene if needed. Amanda, Bruce, and Burdi stood behind him with their mouths open.

Ben simply shook his head, letting Pete know to not get involved.

"Dad," Olivia said again, hoping to get his gaze back on her.

Her father slowly lowered his hands from Ben's neck. "The transplant," he said weakly.

Olivia shook her head slowly.

Without another word, her father pushed past her and disappeared into the kitchen.

"I'll go talk to him. Are you okay?"

"I'm fine," Ben said as he rubbed his neck. He looked stunned and a little guilty.

"I love you," she whispered firmly to him before following her father.

Olivia found him in the half-finished kitchen with his back to her, his hands resting on a steel countertop. Her boots slid across the dust-capped tile as she walked toward him.

"I'm going to talk for a minute and I want you to listen." She dragged her hand across the smooth surface of a steel shelf.

Her father grunted and shifted his feet. Olivia continued, taking small steps toward him. Her fingers jumped to the island in the center of the kitchen.

"First of all, I'm just as much to blame for this as Ben... both of us had a part in it." It felt patronizing, but it needed to be said. He shouldn't have gone after Ben like that.

His broad shoulders seemed to grow bigger, like a huge stone wall she couldn't breach. But she continued, hoping her words would surge over his cold barrier.

"Remember how I wanted to be a marine biologist when I was a kid? The idea of breathing underwater and exploring a different world sounded so... magical. But as I got older and my health got worse, I realized that wasn't realistic. I guess dreams don't always come true and life doesn't always go as you plan."

Olivia paused as she took a deep breath with her last step. She was standing right behind him but he wouldn't turn around. So stubborn, she thought.

"What is it that John Lennon said? *Life is what happens to you while you're busy making other plans?*"

She turned and rested her backside against the counter and lean over to see his face. His eyes shifted to hers for a moment, then away again. I can talk all day, mister, she thought.

"I have the chance to leave something behind that I never planned... never even dreamed," she corrected. "I have the chance to leave a little piece of me."

As she spoke, she realized she was finally putting all her thoughts together, like beads on a string. Now, she understood her crazy. Smiling, she put her hand on her stomach.

The corner of her father's mouth turned up and his eyes softened. He was starting to crack so she pulled out his Christmas present. She needed the ammo.

She slid the envelope across the counter toward him. "Inside are two passes for a tour of the Library of Congress. You've always talked about going and I want to spend more time with you. Just the two of us."

Her father looked up, tears rolling down his cheeks, and he pulled her into his chest. She felt like a child again, just happy to be loved and in her father's arms.

"I hate that this disease cheated you of a normal life," he said in between gasps. "I don't want to let you go. You're my world, Olivia."

She had only seen her father cry once, at her mother's funeral. His pain bled into her and all she could do was nod into his chest.

"I'm your father. I'm supposed to protect you from everything. But I can't protect you from this," he sobbed.

His words crushed her heart and she didn't know how to respond. Tears gave way and rolled down her cheeks. All she could think to do was hug him tight and say: "I love you to the moon and back."

"To the moon and back," he replied.

Olivia's father poured coffee from a thermos into mugs and began passing them around. He still hadn't completely thawed out but the party had significantly warmed up despite its rocky start.

Leaning back in a creaking wooden chair, Olivia rubbed behind Teddy Roosevelt's ears. "I don't think I can eat another bite," she said and pushed her half-eaten pie away. Teddy lifted his head and sniffed.

"You have to eat through the pain," Pete said as he shoved the last bit of apple pie into his mouth.

"Where did you get this pie, Dad?"

"Yeah, it's delicious," Amanda said through a mouthful.

"What if I told you I made it?" He plopped down onto a metal stool.

"I wouldn't believe you," Olivia quipped.

"I would," Ben retorted.

Olivia covered her mouth and smiled. Ben was doing everything in his power to get back in her father's good graces. But she knew it wouldn't work. Not yet anyway. Her father just needed time.

"Alright, alright. Nancy from next door brought it over," he replied.

"Oh la la, Nancy," Amanda teased.

"Oh, stop it," her father said with a wave of his hand. Although, he couldn't hide the smile that spread across his lips.

"Who's Nancy?" Burdi asked.

"She's been our neighbor for nearly ten years," Olivia explained to the table.

"She's just a friend," her father added.

"Friendships turn into the best relationships," Pete said and gave a thumbs up to Ben.

Olivia's father frowned but Pete didn't seem to notice. Instead, he draped his arm around the back of Amanda's chair and changed the subject. "So, when are we singing Christmas carols?"

"You don't want to hear this one sing," Bruce said, nudging Burdi.

She gave him a gentle slap on his arm and giggled.

"How about, *Grandma Got Run Over by a Reindeer?* Pete suggested.

"That is literally the worst Christmas song ever written," Amanda protested.

"I beg to differ," Pete mumbled.

"*The Little Drummer Boy?*" Bruce suggested.

"There's no way I know all the words to that song," Olivia said.

"You know," Bruce cleared his throat. "Come little drummer boy pa rum pum pum...This boy's the new-found king..." Bruce's voice quickly faded away as he lost the lyrics.

"That's not how it goes!" laughed Burdi.

"Jingle Bells," Amanda pitched in. "Everyone knows Jingle Bells and you can't screw it up."

The rest of the evening continued just like that: debating over which song to sing, singing a bar or two, and then arguing over who sang it wrong. Snow sprinkled down from the dark sky as they sat warm and comfortable in the half-finished restaurant. Olivia looked around at all their faces and silently begged for time to stop.

CHAPTER EIGHTEEN
The Final Countdown

Olivia stood sideways in front of a full-length mirror as she carefully zipped up the side of her dress. She, Amanda, and Burdi had taken solace in the hotel's bridal suite to change after spending the last five hours setting up for the company holiday party. With one more deep breath in, she forced the zipper closed.

At only 12 weeks, her breasts were already much bigger. But beyond that, not much had changed, except that she was constantly eating. She had to. When she wasn't pregnant, she was barely getting enough calories as it were. Now, she had to double it.

She sprayed some perfume on the insides of her wrists and just under her neck. Her dogwood bracelet reflected off the antique chandelier above and onto her skin. Behind her, Amanda came waddling out of the en-suite bathroom as she tried to adjust the padded bra Burdi made her buy.

"This is absurd. I should take it off right?" Amanda asked.

Before Olivia could respond, the suite door burst open. Burdi was in the middle of an intense conversation with Natalie. As she crossed the room, her robe fluttered, revealing a black garter underneath.

"I don't care if he said there's a chance of snow," Burdi said. "I'm paying him to be my florist, not my weatherman. I want the flowers and lights I ordered on the balcony, even if no one ends up going outside."

"Absolutely," Natalie replied without intonation as she scribbled down some notes on a clipboard. "I couldn't agree more." She turned and quickly disappeared from the room.

"What time is it?" Burdi asked no one in particular as she slipped off her robe.

"Quarter to eight," Olivia said as she put in a diamond earring.

"We have fifteen minutes! Help me into my dress!"

Olivia looked at Amanda and pointed to her earring. "I'm busy," she whispered.

"Oh, how convenient," Amanda mumbled.

She took a swig out of a glass tumbler before walking over to Burdi and Olivia stifled a laugh. As soon as Burdi was zipped in, she smoothed out the red princess flare skirt and turned to look in the mirror.

"Nope!" she said as she tried to reach for the zipper at the back of the dress. "No, no, no! Get me out if it!"

"What the...?" Amanda mumbled and took a step back from her.

"Burdi, deep breaths. The tonight's going to be perfect," Olivia reassured her.

"No, it's not that." She dropped her hands to her sides. "Bruce wants to fly to Vegas tonight and elope. And like an idiot, I said yes!" Burdi looked back-and-forth between them but Amanda and Olivia just stared at her. "I said yes!" she repeated, then started pacing. "What was I thinking? I can't get married again!"

Amanda shrugged. "What's the big deal? I hear third time's the charm."

Olivia sent her an exasperated look before turning to Burdi. "Bruce is an amazing guy," she said.

"He's such an amazing guy," Burdi said dreamily without looking at her. "I don't deserve him."

"Yeah, you know, he really is..." Amanda said, wrinkling her brow.

"Of course you deserve him," Olivia said over Amanda.

"But me and marriage..." Burdi started fanning herself. "I ruin it every time."

"At least that's something you can control. Unlike someone who cheats..." Amanda took another gulp of her drink.

"Not helping," Olivia said through clenched teeth before turning back to Burdi. "Look, I know you've had bad experiences in the past but you can't let that decide your future." Olivia pulled her over to the couch and sat down. "Are you in love with him?"

Burdi looked at her, surprised. "Of course."

"Will you love him until the day you die?"

"Yes."

"And do you trust that he feels the same?"

"Yes, but—"

"Do you want to be right or do you want to be happy?"

"Hey, that's my line," Amanda said as she crunched on an ice cube.

Burdi shrugged. "Happy... I want to be happy," she finally said with a smile. "But I think I need a drink first."

"That a girl." Amanda pointed to her like they'd just coached a player to success. "I'll get you a double."

Olivia followed her over to the wet bar.

"Nice speech," Amanda mumbled.

"It's good advice."

"Yeah, well, we need to start taking our own advice," she added wearily as she reached for a tumbler.

Olivia paused as she unscrewed the cap of a water bottle. "Yeah..." she muttered.

"Bacon wrapped date?" A waiter presented his tray to Olivia. "Yes please," she said. Her eyes gleamed like a child being offered candy without her parent's permission. She popped the morsel into her mouth. The sweet, salty combination danced on her tongue. "Maybe I'll grab another..." She greedily seized another just as a pair of strong arms wrapped around her waist.

"Hey, beautiful. Can I buy you a drink?" Ben's breath tickled her ear.

She smiled and turned to face him. "I got you one of these," she lied.

"Sure you did. How about you keep that one for the baby."

Her breath caught in her chest. "I don't think I'll ever get used to you saying that."

They joined hands and moved through the crowded ballroom. Cocktail tables and lounge seating adorned in silver and gold circled the dance floor, with a DJ, photo booth, and fully stocked bar posted close by. The outward facing walls were not even walls at all but floor-to-ceiling windows that offered a 180-degree view of Washington D.C.

"Here you go, kid," Pete said as he handed Olivia a Shirley Temple and Ben a glass of bourbon. "I had them put it in a martini glass so you look cool."

"Thanks," she grumbled.

"You know, this reminds me of our first date," Pete said to Amanda.

"First and last date," Amanda corrected before turning to Olivia and Ben. "What possessed you two to think it would be a good idea for me to bring him to my cousin's wedding? What a disaster."

"You're a disaster!" Pete said.

"Seriously? How old are you?"

"I gave you the time of your life," Pete mumbled as *I Wanna Dance with Somebody* started bumping through the speakers.

"I know how you can make it up to me." Amanda set her drink down on the bar. "Let's dance."

Pete raised his eyebrows and looked at her as if she'd just offered to do a line of cocaine with him in the bathroom.

Without waiting for an answer, Amanda grabbed his hand and pulled him toward the dance floor.

As Olivia watched them, she started to wonder if this was Amanda's way of taking her own advice. *But Amanda and Pete?* She shook her head. *No way.*

"Look at what we started," Ben said as he wrapped his arm around her shoulders.

"Don't speak too soon. Those two are a ticking time bomb."

"They're no worse than us," he said with a smile.

Ben and Olivia showed off their stiff box step as they moved across the floor to Etta James. Olivia's head rested against Ben's collarbone as he held her tight.

"Aren't you glad we took dance lessons? We're creaming these old folks."

Olivia laughed. "I didn't know this was a competition."

"If Bifocals over there doesn't stop eyeing you, there will be words."

She looked over to see the oldest man in the room, hunched over in a chair. He had more wrinkles than strands of hair.

Olivia gave Ben a playful slap. "That's our oldest client! He was Burdi's first sale!" she whispered.

"I can tell," Ben said, still staring down the old man.

Olivia smiled and rested her head back down on his shoulder. She watched the couples around them, completely consumed by their partner. Each pair fit together perfectly like they were made for each other. They moved together in comfortable unison as if they could handle whatever step came next.

Love used to seem like a foreign concept to Olivia, something she would never understand. But now she did. She was one of the lucky ones who found it. She was a part of this group. She was madly in love too.

The song ended and the DJ's booming voice came through the speakers. "Alright, alright everyone. It's that time of the night." The wait staff appeared and handed out glasses of champagne, party hats, noisemakers, and glow sticks. "The new year is just a few minutes away!"

Olivia was afraid to marry Ben because she wanted to do it for the right reasons and at the right time. But she didn't have time and who cared about it being right? They'd been doing it all wrong from the start. *I don't want to be right. I want to be happy*, she thought.

Olivia's heart started to pound rapidly against her chest. "I need air," she said to Ben and pulled him through the crowded dance floor and out onto the balcony.

The sharp, frigid air made her lungs seize as soon as she stepped outside. Snow fell in giant chunks and stuck to her hair in big flakes. The balcony railing was wrapped in lighted rope and tall flower arrangements dotted each corner. Two heat lamps faced each other at a diagonal in the middle but did little to warm the exposed terrace.

"It's freezzzinnggg," she said with a shiver.

Ben took off his jacket and draped it over her shoulders. "What was your first clue?" he said with a laugh as he gestured to the snow falling around them.

She smiled slightly and wrapped the jacket around her body.

"What's going on?" Ben asked.

The DJ's muffled voice bled onto the balcony: "Thirty seconds!"

"This is insane," she mumbled and looked down at her feet. *But maybe it's supposed to be*, she thought. *Maybe that's what love does. It blinds you from sanity.*

"Olivia," Ben pressed.

"I want forever with you," she said. "I want you, our kid, a white picket fence, and a stick figure family on the back of our car." A single tear rolled down her cheek, burning her skin as it met the cold air.

"You have me, Olivia," he said, furrowing his brow.

"You once shouted that you loved me on a rooftop. You wanted to the world to know. I want the world to know that I love you too." She paused and took a deep breath. "Will you marry me?"

A single "HAPPY NEW YEAR!" followed by muffled cheers and applause erupted from inside the hotel ballroom. Ben cheered along with them.

"Yes!" he yelled. He picked Olivia up and spun her around.

She laughed and kissed him deeply.

"Hold on."

He put her down and reached under her right arm into his jacket pocket. When his hand reappeared, he was holding a small velvet black box.

Olivia's eyes widened. "What is that?" She was shaking, but she wasn't sure if it was from the cold anymore.

He opened the box to reveal a sparkling oval diamond ring.

She recognized it immediately. "Is that…"

"It was your mother's. Your dad gave it to me."

"When?" she asked, unable to hide her surprise.

"A few days ago. He came around a lot faster than I thought." He started to slide the ring onto her finger but then stopped. "No stick figure family. Deal?"

"Deal," she said with a laugh.

He smiled and slid the ring onto Olivia's finger. They kissed again, a lingering, knee-weakening kiss, and Olivia felt like she could hold him forever.

CHAPTER NINETEEN
The Right Place

Olivia stared at the bike path in front of her. A group of cyclists in racing gear whizzed by without a bell or word. Her head throbbed and her limbs felt like Jell-O but she did all she could to ignore the tiny voice in her head, begging her to go home and sleep.

After fighting off a bad case of bronchitis, being outside hospital walls felt strange but liberating. The late March air was cool and damp. It had been a while since Olivia had felt fresh air in her lungs and the sun on her cheeks.

She ran a lot in her early twenties, enough to successfully complete a dozen races. Dr. Katz had told her it would help increase her lung function and energy levels. But when she turned 25 she came down with a serious lung infection and couldn't seem to find the same energy or motivation to get back into the routine again.

Olivia looked down at her swollen belly. Her health had been the only thing on her mind lately. She needed to be as active as possible and consume at least 3,500 good calories a day.

"Just do enough to feel your heart pumping and the burn in your lungs again," her dietitian had told her.

That shouldn't be a problem.

Olivia took a puff from her inhaler then pushed her right foot forward. Appointments with Dr. Katz, obstetrician checkups, and ultrasounds ran in a loop every month. Her doctors were all concerned about the same things: her vulnerability to infections, the amount of nutrition getting to the baby, and her restricted airflow as the baby grew. The monotony was exhausting.

She reached a bridge next to some soccer fields and took a hard left up a hill roofed by tall white pines. She had already started to sweat and the shade brought a welcome relief from the sun.

Her wedding was in a month. By then she'll be 29 weeks pregnant. Olivia cringed as she imagined herself in a loose-fitting white dress, unable to hide the bulge at her center. She'd already started to endure the whispers and questions from co-workers and acquaintances. *Is she pregnant? How long have they been dating? Are they getting married?* She didn't have the energy or the patience to explain her situation to everyone, nor did she care to. The people who mattered knew and she was more than happy to leave it that way.

She took a big gulp from her water bottle as she approached a break in the trail. A neighborhood street crossed over the bike path and she took a left to follow it.

Olivia didn't just choose the Arlington side of the W&OD trail for its looks. She had ulterior motives for leaving Washington D.C. for the quaint Virginia burrow. She wanted to think of something other than her health for a change.

All the houses on the block were brick colonial-style but each carried its own personality. Some were painted white with dark blue shutters and some were uncovered brick with ivy. Some had screened-in porches while others had two-story additions in the back.

Olivia stopped in front of the smallest house on the street with a "For Sale" sign planted in the front yard. A real estate friend of Burdi's told her about the home and Olivia jumped at the opportunity to take a look. It was a quaint three bedroom, two and a half bath brick rambler with a screened-in porch off the left side. Black shutters and trim decorated its face and large bushes lined its base. There seemed to be minimal landscaping to maintain, which was comforting. She knew it would be hard for Ben to keep up with it by himself.

Olivia pushed the thought away as she opened the lockbox. It was something she'd come to realize when they started looking for a place together. At the end of the day, the house would be for Ben and their child, not her.

She opened the front door and stepped inside. The house had been freshly painted for the sale and had a surprising open concept and high ceilings for its age. The kitchen wasn't modern but it was simple and clean. She made her way to the back of the house. The master was small but had an en-suite bathroom. Down the hall was a Jack-and-Jill bathroom with pink and black tile.

Whoa. That's intense, Olivia thought as she continued to the next bedroom. *And this carpet has got to go...*

She sighed. *Maybe I'm being too critical,* Olivia thought as she entered the second bedroom. Ben sold his condo in February and they were going crazy in her small studio apartment.

Instead, she focused on her priorities: not too big, easy to maintain, good school district, and, coupled with her life insurance policy, affordable for one income. So far, the house seemed to meet every requirement.

She stopped in the middle of the bedroom and looked around. Sunlight poured in through a bay window and bright green trees from the fenced-in backyard waved back-and-forth inside its frame. Her mind drifted as she imagined filling the room with a crib, curtains, and a rocking chair.

Olivia leaned a hand against the bay window's frame and looked out across the lawn when, suddenly, her eyes darted to the back fence. In the far corner of the yard was a dogwood tree. And, as if on cue, a tumbling motion erupted in her belly. She gasped and her hand flew to her stomach. She felt a kick. The very first kick.

✳ ✳ ✳

Dr. Kim smeared cold goo on Olivia's exposed stomach and she shivered. Ben should be here. She needed him here and she couldn't help but feel a twinge of resentment toward him. But the restaurant was vying for its liquor license and he told her he would be late. She'd debated calling her father or Amanda to come along but ultimately decided to go alone and feel sorry for herself.

It's the hormones, she told herself and bounced her feet anxiously.

Dr. Kim glided what looked like a vacuum cleaner detachment over her stomach. Faint black and white shapes came in and out of focus on a nearby monitor but for blinking seconds, Olivia could see the outline of a tiny baby. Numbers lined the side of the monitor, adjusting with each shift of Dr. Kim's hand, as a wonky thumping sound pumped through the speakers. Olivia held her breath, waiting for the assessment.

"Your baby looks great, Olivia. Really," Dr. Kim said. "The fetus is a little bit bigger than the size of my hand now." She turned to Olivia and held up her hand, smiling. Her teeth were perfectly white and her black hair shone in the fluorescent lights.

Olivia figured she was supposed to "oh" and "aww" at the comparison but she didn't have the compulsion. She was just happy to hear the baby was okay. "That's great," she replied.

It was apparently good enough for Dr. Kim because she turned back to the screen. "Your baby is on the lower end of the weight range I prefer to see by this time but your baby is within range," she continued. "Just keep up those calories, okay?"

Olivia nodded worthlessly to the back of Dr. Kim's head as she continued to stare at the sonogram.

"Would you like to know the sex of your baby? I think we might get a good look today."

"Oh," she said in surprise. She hadn't expected this. She always imagined she and Ben would find out together and she didn't want to take the moment away from him.

"I'm here! I made it!" Ben came charging into the room. "How does our baby look?"

"Perfect timing," Dr. Kim said without taking her eyes off the monitor. "Everything looks good. I was just asking Olivia: would you like to know the sex of your baby?"

Ben looked at Olivia. His face was a mixture of excitement and panic. "What do you think?" he asked her. "Do you want to know?"

Olivia nodded. She didn't need to give the reason why. Everyone in the room knew she might not survive the birth to meet her child.

Ben smiled. "Well, I'm in." He grabbed her hand.

Olivia's heart was pumping a mile a minute as she anxiously watched the screen and Dr. Kim. She could feel her breath leave her nose in perforated bursts.

Dr. Kim turned to face them. "Ben and Olivia... you're having a baby girl." She flashed another toothpaste commercial smile.

A girl! Tingling warmth spread through Olivia's body. She looked up at Ben as a huge smile made its way across her lips.

He beamed back at her. "A girl, Olivia!" He took her face and planted a soft, swift kiss on her lips.

She was giddy with excitement—the real excitement she should've had when she first found out she was pregnant. And Ben was here to share in it.

For some reason, knowing the sex of her child made it so much more real. It was really happening. She was having a baby girl.

CHAPTER TWENTY
Eagle's Wings

The light grey concrete was cracked and riddled with tiny stones. Olivia held her portable oxygen tank, concealed in her green purse, tight to her body as she shuffled along the narrow path. An old man with his own oxygen tank a few yards away turned to look at her with uninterested eyes. She smiled and waved to him in solidarity. He frowned before turning away and marching down a steep hill.

She figured it wasn't every day you saw a pregnant woman with an oxygen tank. When the tank became a permanent accessory last week, Olivia complained to Ben that she probably looked like a pregnant geriatric patient. "Should I get you some Depends?" he had asked with a laugh.

A cold breeze pushed the hair off Olivia's shoulders and she hugged herself for warmth. She was cold and uncomfortable but pushed her feet forward anyway. *Get used to it*, she told herself. *These are your future neighbors.*

Headstones tessellated around her in rows and columns. She looked up at the sky and saw grey billowing clouds moving quickly overhead. "I swear it was just sunny," Olivia mumbled. It was as if visiting a cemetery must include an ominous sky and violent gusts of wind.

She peeled off her sunglasses and headed towards a large willow tree. She watched as the long hanging branches stretched to the ground like fingers, swaying delicately in the wind. They beckoned her, pulling her closer.

Olivia had never visited her grave before. The last time she was here was the day of her funeral but she remembered the spot exactly. It had been seared into her memory and she'd visited it in her mind often over the years.

Adjacent to the willow tree was a small, dark grey headstone. An angel leaned over its face, offering protection from the elements with its petite body and splaying wings. Olivia knelt down and dusted off the pollen and dirt from the granite face.

JANE HAMMEL

Loving wife & mother

1952 - 1996

Away I fly on eagle's wings

She remembered the song. It was her mother's favorite. Her parents had taken Olivia to services as a kid. Whenever the song played, her mother would close her eyes and belt the words:

And He will raise you up on eagle's wings
Bear you on the breath of dawn
Make you to shine like the sun
And hold you in the palm of His hand

After she died, Olivia had so many questions and still didn't have all the answers. The police had said her mother hit black ice, overcorrected and crashed into a guardrail going 60 miles an hour. She was on her way home.

Olivia had been mad at her mother for so long. Why did she have to drive that night? Why couldn't she have just gone for a walk? But when she thought of her mother now she didn't think of the last time she saw her. She only remembered her smile, how she laughed, and the way her hands felt. She was warm and comforting, spontaneous and lively.

One morning, when Olivia was six, her mother woke her up at dawn and drove her to the Baltimore Aquarium. It was a school day but her mother said: "Everyone deserves a day off every now and then, especially if they don't waste it." They spent hours with their faces pressed up against thick tank glass, watching the underwater life pass by in a kaleidoscope of colors.

Olivia's vision refocused to the cold stone in front of her. She'd gotten so lost in her thoughts that she'd forgotten she was still kneeling in front of her mother's headstone.

Reaching the end of her life had caused Olivia to reevaluate everything she'd done. Her mother had tried so hard to do everything right, while Olivia felt like she had tried too little. Good or bad, satisfied or unsatisfied, she was learning to come to terms with it.

Olivia swiveled her head to the left and then to the right. She was alone. It was time to do what she came here to do.

"So… a lot's been going on…" She said as she patted her stomach. "I'm pregnant. It's a girl… And, don't worry. I'm marrying the father soon. It's Ben. You don't know him but I think you would've liked him."

Another violent gust of wind blew past her. She could smell rain in the air and knew she needed to hurry.

"And, um, I'll probably die pretty soon after that. I gave up a lung transplant to have the baby so… Does it hurt? Does dying hurt?"

Olivia felt foolish as she stared at the silent grey marble. She silently begged for an answer or a sign but knew it would never come. Pressure began to build behind her eyes.

"I wish you were here," she continued. "You always knew what to say… But you're not here and I'm still mad at you about that. You carried the world on your shoulders and you never let dad or me share the burden. But I wish you had. We were stronger together but you left us. And without you, we're incomplete." Tears filled the corners of her eyes and she took a deep breath. "You were the most beautiful person I knew, inside and out. You were my hero."

This pain wouldn't end with Olivia. Her daughter would have to live without her mother too and she hated that she was passing along that pain. She cupped her hand over her mouth as she cried, trying to stifle the sound.

Despite being alone, she was embarrassed for getting so emotional. She brushed the tears from her cheeks. "Anyway... I wish I had told you that," she said, her voice still shaking.

Olivia touched her hand to her lips then pressed her hand to the cold stone. "I love you and miss you so much, Mom," she whispered before lifting herself off the ground. "And if Ben's right, I'll see you soon."

✳ ✳ ✳

Olivia yanked a stiff roll of packing tape across a large cardboard box. It had only taken her, Ben, Amanda and her father an afternoon to pack up almost all of her belongings. Her body ached and she was ready for a nap.

Pete sat nearby on a stool with his feet on the countertop. "How about Beyoncé? Now that's a fierce name," he said as he popped bubble wrap between his fingers. He'd been rattling off every celebrity he could think of to help them pick a name for the baby.

Amanda walked over to Pete and ripped the bubble wrap from his hands. "You're driving me crazy!"

Pete smiled. "Love you too."

"How about Eleanor?" Olivia's father suggested. Like Pete, Olivia's father had been calling out famous names. Except, instead of celebrity names, he'd been suggesting names of famous female historical figures.

Ben made a face and shook his head behind her father.

"No," Olivia said delicately.

Minkus hid in an empty box next to her and she teased him with her fingers. His paw sprung out and then slowly disappeared inside the box again.

"We all know her name is going to be Amanda anyway. Right, Olivia?" Amanda beamed at her as she placed a stack of carefully wrapped dishes in a cardboard box.

Pete let out an exaggerated laugh. "In your dreams."

"I think I have a name in mind, actually," Olivia said as she stacked a pile of books. Everyone's eyes focused on Olivia as they waited for her to continue. She paused for a moment, secretly enjoying the suspense. "How about Jane?" she finally said.

"Jane…" Ben said, smiling. "It's perfect."

CHAPTER TWENTY-ONE
Normal for a Moment

"I'm not coming back next year. I just can't keep up with all my classes when I keep getting sick."

Ben sat on her bed across from her looking devastated. He wore a tattered PKA t-shirt and sweatpants as if he'd just gotten out of bed. The two sat alone in Olivia's dorm room, her pictures and posters already removed from the walls in anticipation of summer break. The warm late spring air wafted through the room and brought the sounds of students laughing and playing football on the lawn.

They weren't dating. They might have made out once when they were both drunk but nothing official. So, why was it so hard to tell him she was leaving?

"What are you going to do?" he asked.

"I'm not sure... I might try community college. There's a little bit more flexibility there."

Ben lifted his hand then returned it to his lap again. Olivia could tell he didn't know what to say or do. They'd seen each other almost every day for the past two years. Now, like ripping off a band-aid, he wouldn't be around all the time. The thought made Olivia feel sick to her stomach.

"We'll stay in touch, right?" she asked, hoping she didn't sound desperate.

"I'll always be around." He took Olivia's hand and put it in his. "I'm not going anywhere."

She closed her eyes, enjoying his touch. When she opened them again, Ben was looking right at her. His gaze was intense and smoldering. He started to tilt his body toward her, keeping his eyes open and locked on hers. Olivia stayed still and watched him come closer. He smelled like aftershave, spicy and fresh.

She knew he wanted to kiss her and that terrified her. She was leaving college and never coming back. People always said they would stay in touch but they never did. She was sure Ben would eventually move on and forget about her and she didn't want to get her heart broken.

Olivia sprung up from the bed. She refused to look at him but she knew his face was clouded with humiliation and confusion. She walked over to her closet and pretended to continue packing as if she hadn't noticed the sexual tension hanging heavy in the room.

Better to be safe than sorry, *she reasoned.*

✳ ✳ ✳

If Olivia regretted one moment in her life it was the day she left Ben heartbroken in her empty dorm room. If she'd kissed him, they might have gotten it right. They would have taken their time, dated for a few years, gotten married, and bought a house. Then, they would plan a family when the time was right—everything in the right order. The way it was supposed to go.

Instead, she was standing 29 weeks pregnant in a loose chiffon wedding gown in the office above Ben's restaurant. An oxygen line wrapped around her face and disappeared under her dress. For someone who had never thought about her wedding day before, she was surprised that disappointment weighed heavy in her gut. It all just seemed lackluster and rushed.

Olivia had convinced Ben to treat their wedding as a dry run for the restaurant. The opening was in two weeks and it seemed like the perfect opportunity to test recipes and work out any service kinks. Plus, Ben's menu reflected his roots growing up in Louisiana and Olivia loved his beignets.

Thirty of their closest friends and family awaited her descent down the grand staircase. Ben's parents even made it.

Is it normal to be nervous? Or is it a bad sign? she thought as she bit the end of her thumb and tapped her foot.

Her father pulled her thumb away from her face and placed his hands over hers to still them. "You look so beautiful, honey." He squeezed her hands.

"About ready?" Amanda asked as she fluffed Olivia's dress from the back.

Olivia nodded.

"Oh! I almost forgot!" Amanda hopped over Olivia's train. Her strapless navy chiffon dress bounced dangerously high on her thighs.

She took a small wooden box off the desk and opened it to reveal a glimmer of blue and white: her mother's hair comb. "Dad, will you do the honors?" She handed Olivia's father the comb and he gently secured it into the side of Olivia's head.

"Okay, your oxygen tank is at the top of the stairs," Amanda continued. "You have enough line to make it down the stairs to say your vows but we'll have to move the tank for the reception."

Olivia scrunched her face. Now that the baby had grown, it had gotten harder for Olivia to breathe—as if that were possible. She'd been forced to shackle herself to a larger tank and could only use her portable one if she would only be out of the house for a few hours.

Amanda circled around to face her, reading the apprehension on her face. "Don't worry. No one will notice," she assured her.

Olivia smiled unconvincingly, her oxygen line pulling on her cheeks. "Okay, I'm ready," she said.

Amanda cracked open the office door and waved her hand. The sound of a grand piano playing a slow ballad made its way up to the office.

"Here we go," Amanda said before grabbing her simple bouquet of yellow roses and slipping out the door.

Olivia turned to her father. "Ready?"

"How about just for the ceremony?" He gently released the loops around her ears and pulled the tubes away from her face.

"Thank you," she whispered. "Thank you for everything." Her bottom lip quivered as she helped him pull the oxygen line out from under her dress.

When they reached the landing, Olivia took a moment to breathe. The banister was wrapped with a green leaf garland and yellow roses. Amanda and Pete flanked the bottom of the stairs and smiled up at her. Behind them, guests sat at round tables scattered around the restaurant. Flashes from cameras reached her eyes and boggled her vision.

Olivia looked down the staircase and, suddenly, all she could see was Ben. She smiled, comforted just by the sight of him. He stood next to the Officiant in a grey suit and looked up at her with a warm smile and soft eyes. He looked like a man in love.

The pressure from the baby alone was enough to make Olivia winded, so she knew she needed to take her time. She nodded to her father and with his support, they carefully began their decent. Her ankles shook beneath her as she tried to keep herself steady.

By the time they reached the bottom, Olivia was breathing hard but she ignored the strain in her chest. Her Cystic Fibrosis wasn't going steal her attention. Not today.

"Welcome, family, friends and loved ones," the Officiant began. "We gather here today to celebrate the marriage of Ben and Olivia..."

She clasped Ben's hands. They were warm and comforting, while hers were cold and clammy. His warmth spread through her fingertips to the rest of her body and all her tension melted away. She looked up at him and his lips pulled back into an even bigger grin.

Their story didn't unfold the way she thought it was supposed to or the way she expected. But it didn't matter how they got here. She was just glad they finally did.

CHAPTER TWENTY-TWO
Potato Chips and Ranch

Leaning over her kitchen island, Olivia dipped a ruffled potato chip into a small bowl of ranch dressing and popped the morsel into her mouth. Good Lord, that's good, she thought as she squirted maple syrup over some chunky peanut butter on rye bread.

Minkus' ears shifted forward at the sound as he sat judging her from the windowsill. Olivia ignored him and added a few pickles before folding the soft bread over itself and taking a big bite. If only I could have some wine. She looked down at her belly then up to her portable oxygen tank resting on the island. She glared at the tank as if it was her kidnapper holding her captive.

Tonight was the restaurant opening and Olivia had gotten hungry while waiting for Ben to pick her up because he "refused to let his pregnant wife drive all the way into DC." Like it's far. She rolled her eyes remembering their argument. It ended with Olivia shouting at him to stop treating her like she was made of glass and slamming the bedroom door.

Her doctors had recently put her on "modified bed rest," which turned out to be easier than expected. Her life had already consisted mostly of sleep and medical treatments. But she didn't feel like she had a life anymore and was becoming more and more irritable because of it.

Guilt stung Olivia deep in her chest. All week, Ben had been running himself ragged getting everything ready for the restaurant, unpacking boxes, and waiting on her hand-and-foot. Whether it was rubbing her feet or running to get ice cream, he did it without hesitation. She was so grateful for everything he did for her and she wondered if she'd ever told him that.

They'd been married for 16 days. Nothing felt different and marriage didn't solve her problems but now she could take comfort in the fact that she knew, without a shadow of a doubt, that she had someone who loved her and would always be by her side. She glanced at the glimmering diamond on her left hand. Olivia Luckette. It still sounded like a dream.

Just then, Ben came bursting through the front door. "Honey, I'm home!" he called.

Olivia smiled and shook her head. "I'm in the kitchen!" she called back.

Ben walked up behind her and wrapped his strong arms around her waist. She melted into his touch. "How are you feeling?" he asked.

"Tired," Olivia admitted. "Your girl has been dancing all day." She patted her stomach.

"That's my girl," he said and leaned over her shoulder.

"Crunchy peanut butter and syrup on rye bread—"

"And pickles."

"Well, it's definitely not your worst. What do you call it?"

"Dul-i-ch-ush," she said through a mouthful of sandwich.

"Sexy." He leaned in and kissed her forehead. "Now, this combination," he paused to dip a chip in the bowl of ranch. "*This* is delicious."

"I'll let you steal the idea for your restaurant."

"*Our* restaurant," he corrected. "Speaking of: you do know there will be food there, right?"

"It's not my fault. Jane was hungry." She looked up at him with big, innocent eyes.

"Well, whatever Jane wants, Jane gets."

"We have to be careful or we're going to spoil this little girl." Olivia dusted off her hands and started to clear off the island.

"That's not the plan?"

Ben took the peanut butter from her and put it on the top shelf of the pantry where it belonged. Ever since they started living together, she noticed that they moved around each other like planets, in a rhythmic and logical pattern. They were like two parts of the same machine, moving separately but for the same purpose. It was these little moments that reminded her that they belonged together and they just wouldn't work the same apart.

"Ben?"

"Hmm?" he mumbled as he licked syrup from his fingers.

"Between me, the baby and the restaurant, you've been amazing. I don't know what I would do without you. So, thank you. I don't think I say it enough."

"You're welcome." He leaned down and kissed her lips. "Loving you makes it easy."

She smiled and put the pickles back in the fridge. When she turned around again, Ben was holding his keys in the air.

"Ready to see the restaurant?" he asked mischievously.

With her eyes closed, Olivia took careful steps as Ben led her by the hand. One arm stretched out in front of her as she tried to feel her way through the darkness. She could hear the rush of cars pass by as they walked to the front of the restaurant.

"You will be on death row if you let a pregnant woman fall," she said.

"Trust, Olivia. Trust." He slowed his pace to a complete stop and untangled his arm from hers. "Ready?"

"Ready."

"Okay, open your eyes."

Olivia's vision adjusted to the brick façade of the restaurant. She looked up to see a deep red awning and a sign that read, Olivia's, in big cursive letters. She gasped.

"You named the restaurant after me?" She looked at Ben in shock then turned back to the sign. "I can't... Ben..." she stammered. "Thank you." She wrapped her arms around his neck and kissed him. The oxygen line pulled on her face making it hard to dive in.

"You're welcome."

"I hope Pete wasn't too disappointed. What was it he wanted? *The Rat Tail*?"

"It was always going to be Olivia's. He knew that." He took her hand and led her toward the door. "Come on. Let's get you some food."

As soon as they crossed the threshold, they were hit with a flurry of activity. They wove through tables, avoiding the waiters and waitresses crisscrossing before them with stacks of food and bottles of wine. Olivia inhaled, taking in the rich, spicy aromas.

The restaurant was elegant but still managed to feel casual and inviting. It had a Bourbon Street vibe, with balcony seating behind an ornate iron gate and upbeat music playing on a grand piano in the back. Almost every table was taken, and the sound of clinking glasses and laughter filled the air.

From a corner booth, Amanda and Pete waved them down. Along the way, Ben stopped to ask a few customers how their food was and introduced Olivia as his wife. He beamed with pride but Olivia felt her cheeks get hot when curious eyes landed on her oxygen tubes then shifted down to her belly.

"Aren't you supposed to be in the kitchen?" Ben asked Pete as they approached the table.

"I just wanted to say hello to your beautiful wife." Pete stood and kissed Olivia's cheek.

"You look great, Olivia. Why are all the good ones taken?"

Amanda pretended to vomit behind him.

Olivia laughed and sat down next to her.

"Hey, guys!" Sofia sprinted over to their table. Her face looked slightly crazed.

"How's everything going?" Ben asked.

"It's great! I'm getting a lot of positive feedback. Everyone loves the jambalaya."

Pete slapped Ben's shoulder. "No thanks required, Ben. You're welcome."

"It's my grandmother's recipe."

"Well, I made it."

"So, you followed directions."

"Exactly. Perfectly I'd like to add."

"How long have you been out of the kitchen?"

Pete looked up at the ceiling and started counting on his fingers.

"Alright, we have to get back to the kitchen now."

Amanda caught Pete's wrist before he could turn away. "Wait! Can we all take a picture before you leave? This is a big moment." She handed her phone to Sofia. "Do you mind?"

"Not at all," Sofia said and set up in front of the table.

Ben and Pete shoved into the booth. Olivia's bulging belly pressed against the table and rattled the glasses as she scooted over.

"Geeze, Olivia, you've gained some weight," Pete teased.

"Haha." She exaggerated a laugh and pulled the oxygen line off her face.

"Okay, on three..." Sofia held up Amanda's phone and they all wrapped their arms around each other. "One, two, three!"

The flash momentarily blinded Olivia and she blinked furiously to get her vision back. "Alright, we have a restaurant to run," Ben said. He and Pete jumped up from the table.

Sofia handed the phone back to Amanda. "I'll go grab your waiter. Have fun tonight, ladies!" she said before running off.

"Burdi, Bruce, and your father should be here soon. I'll be back to check in on you in a little bit," Ben said before leaning down to kiss Olivia's forehead.

"I'll be back to check on you too," Pete mimicked and leaned toward Amanda.

"Get out of here!" She laughed and pushed him away.

Ben and Pete turned and nudged each other playfully as they headed back to the kitchen.

"Oh, this one's totally going in the album," Amanda said looking down at the picture on her phone.

Olivia looped the oxygen line back on her face and tilted her head to see the image. The four of them were huddled together with huge smiles that looked to be right on the edge of laughter.

"What album?" Olivia asked.

"This one," Amanda said as she pulled out a large binder and placed it on the table in front of her. "I was supposed to wait to give this to you, but I just couldn't!" Her face pinched with excitement.

Olivia opened the binder and flipped through the pages. Inside were hundreds of pictures of her, from when she was a baby until now. Every major milestone of her life passed before her eyes and she smiled warmly.

"Everyone helped contribute," Amanda said. "Because word on the street is that you don't think you lived a very impressive life. Hopefully, this will change that."

Tears pooled along Olivia's bottom eyelashes as she turned to the last page. "It's beautiful. Thank you."

"And we can put this picture right here." Amanda put her phone, displaying the photo, on top of the blank last page.

Olivia looked at the picture. She looked happy. Her eyes were bright and a huge smile pulled at her cheeks. Her focus shifted to Ben sitting next to her in the picture.

"He was right in front of me this whole time and I missed it."

"You didn't miss it," Amanda said gently. "You caught him just in time."

Olivia leaned her head on Amanda's shoulder. She wasn't ready for the end. She wished she could jump into the image and live there forever, stopping time in its tracks.

CHAPTER TWENTY-THREE
Sick of Being Sick

Olivia pushed the wheels at her side and tried to round a sharp corner out of the ornate main gallery of the Library of Congress. Her father had managed to snag a wheelchair for the tour. And while the smooth marble flooring made it easy to roll, she kept having trouble with turns.

"Ouch!" Her father exclaimed in a hushed tone after Olivia ran over one of his heels. Again. "If you're going to insist on steering yourself, you better stop running over my feet."

Olivia smiled. "I'm sorry!"

"I can tell," he deadpanned. "Come on, we need to catch up." He stepped behind her and pushed her around the corner and back to the rest of the tour group.

Air rushed past her cheeks, lifting the hair from her shoulders and away from her temples. It felt strange to go fast. Lately, she'd been feeling so fatigued that she did more sitting than walking. Focusing had become difficult too. They were 30 minutes into the tour and she couldn't remember anything the tour guide had said.

Olivia sighed. Instead of fighting it, she let her mind wander. Despite the photo album Amanda gave her, Olivia still felt unsatisfied with her life. She was grateful, of course, but she couldn't help but think that she'd spent too much time—time she didn't have—desperately trying to be normal. But she wasn't normal and never had been. That kind of life just wasn't the hand she'd been dealt. And now, everything was happening so fast. She didn't know how much time she

116

had left and wanted to leave something behind for the one person who will know her the least: Jane.

She wanted to warn her daughter that life goes too fast even when it felt like it was going too slow. That the worst moments in life help you appreciate the good ones. That life never goes the way you plan but you should plan anyway and roll with the punches. These were life lessons Olivia wished she could give Jane throughout her life but she had to somehow give them to her all at once.

"What are you thinking about?"

Olivia broke her trance and looked up at her father. "Shh! I'm trying to listen to our tour guide," she lied and push herself through an archway behind the rest of the group.

"You never were a very good liar."

After a beat, Olivia gave in. "Do you have any regrets?"

His gait slowed as he thought. "Sure," he said. "But I don't regret my regrets. I learned from all of them."

"Well, I do."

"What do you regret?"

"I don't know… I just feel like I didn't do it right. Life, I mean. There was always that ticking clock in the back of my mind and I always ignored it. I knew I didn't have as much time as everyone else but I wasted it anyway."

"Wasted, huh?" He stepped in front of her and put his hands on the wheelchair's armrests. "Olivia, I'm sorry, but you need to get your head out of your ass."

Olivia's mouth fell open in shock.

"There are a lot of people who love you and who are a part of that so-called wasted life of yours," he continued. "Just because your life doesn't look like a Hallmark card doesn't mean you did it all wrong."

Her eyes fell to the floor, shame beginning to close the back of her throat.

"Let me ask you this," he gently touched her elbow, giving her the strength to raise her eyes back to his. "Are you happy?"

"That's a loaded question."

"It's a yes or no question," he countered.

She paused and thought for a moment. She thought of Ben kissing her on a rooftop under the stars, Amanda and Burdi squeezing her hand in the middle of a crowded club, her mother's amazed face as she watched stingrays swim past her at the Baltimore Aquarium, and her father giving her away at her wedding. She had a loving family, great

117

friends, a baby on the way, and a man who loved her.

"Yes, I'm happy," she responded.

"Well, in my opinion, a happy life isn't a wasted life."

"You're right," she conceded.

"I'm always right." He winked at her and set himself upright again. "Now," he said looking around. "Where did our tour group go?"

After the tour, Olivia still felt tired and weak despite sitting in a wheelchair the entire time. She leaned against her father as they sat on a bench outside the Capital, enjoying the warm June air.

"Do you remember the summer you insisted on putting sand in the kitty pool?" he asked. "So you could hide all sorts of treasures in it?"

"I was pretending to be a treasure hunter. I buried some of mom's jewelry in there."

"You gave her a heart attack!" he said with a laugh.

"It needed to feel like the real thing!"

"I hope for your sake Jane won't be as stubborn as you."

"I'm imaginative and resourceful, not stubborn," she replied proudly. "It's funny… I've always felt like a fish out of wat—ouch!" A sudden pain erupted along the lower edge of her stomach.

"What's wrong?" Worry immediately darkened her father's face.

"I think it was just a kick or something. I'm fine." Olivia rubbed the spot where the pain had been. "I think she heard you," she said and elbowed him playfully.

"Hmm, so she *is* just like her mother." He put his arm around her shoulders.

Before Olivia could respond, another intense cramp moved through her and ripped across her stomach. It pulsed then subsided; then pulsed again. *Is this a contraction?* It couldn't be. She was only 34 weeks pregnant.

"Dad." Olivia clutched her stomach as a wave of pain hit her again. She felt like she was going to faint.

"Olivia?" His voice shook with panic.

"I need to get to the hospital. Now."

✳ ✳ ✳

A needle pricked the backside of Olivia's hand and she squeezed Ben's arm. She wanted to yank her hand away but, instead, tried to

118

focus on the whiteboard where her nurse's name was written in cursive: *Calie*.

For three hours, Olivia had been probed and prodded and she just wanted to go home. The hospital smelled like sterilizing alcohol and sour beef stew. Home smelled like lemon and lavender and meant everything was going to be fine. But Dr. Katz and Dr. Kim had agreed that she should be monitored over the weekend. She was having contractions but, apparently, that didn't necessarily mean there was something wrong.

What *was* wrong was her weight and she'd have to be chained to an IV line streaming a nutrition solution until further notice. Her doctors wanted to pump 2,000 additional calories into her body over the next twelve hours as if they were fattening her up for slaughter.

As Calie taped down the IV, Olivia looked over at her father who sat white-faced in a nearby chair. His forearms rested on his thighs and he stared blankly at the floor. He'd been like that for hours.

"Alright, you're set for the night." Calie removed her gloves and tossed them into a nearby bin. "Get some rest."

As soon as she left a deafening silence filled the room.

"Dad…" Olivia said, desperate to break his trance.

He looked up at her and forced a smile. "I'm sorry honey. I'm just tired." He rubbed his eyes before getting up and crossing the room. "I'm going to head home and let you get some rest. I'll be back first thing in the morning." He kissed the top of her head before quickly turning to leave.

He was overwhelmed and Olivia hated that she was giving him that stress. She wasn't worried about herself and the feeling was new for her. Throughout her life, she'd been used to putting herself first because of *her* health, *her* Cystic Fibrosis.

"I need to pee," she announced after a moment and started to get up from the bed. She needed to move, to do something. She held onto her steel IV pole, ready to drag it with her.

"Let me help you." Ben offered his hand as her feet touched down on the cold, grey vinyl floor. "

I'm fine," she said and swatted him away.

"Come on, Olivia, let me help you. Don't be stubborn."

"I've got it," she said through a clenched jaw.

Except, she wasn't so sure she did. Her legs shook violently as she tried to gather the strength to stand. Ben reached for her hand anyway.

"I'm not going to break!"

Olivia plopped back down on the bed and covered her face with her hands. She breathed heavily as all the energy drained from her body. Tubes and wires tangled around her. She felt trapped and desperately wanted to break free. But mostly, she was embarrassed. She was embarrassed for yelling and embarrassed that she couldn't even stand on her own.

"I'm sorry," she said after a moment. "I just… I'm not ready to be a burden to you." Tears immediately filled her eyes as she looked up at him. "I knew the day would come. I just didn't think it would be now."

Ben took her face in her hands. "You will never be a burden to me," he said, looking her square in the eye. "Loving you makes it easy," he reminded her.

A single tear rolled down her right cheek. Why does he understand? Why does he love me? Why couldn't he have fallen in love with a healthy, normal woman? She was so sick of being sick and wanted to scream at the top of her lungs.

Olivia held out her hand to him. It shook violently in the air. "Walk me to the bathroom door?"

He took her hand and gently lifted her from the bed. She leaned against him and felt his strong body press against hers. She wished she could soak up some of his strength for herself. When she finished, he helped her back into bed and tucked her in like a child.

He hovered over her with his arms on either side of her pillow. "I love you," he said. "I'll be right here, all night,"

"Can you lie with me? Just until I fall asleep?" she asked.

He nodded and slipped into the narrow hospital bed next to her.

She shifted, carefully moving her IV out of the way, and folded herself under his arm. With her head on his chest, she concentrated on his breathing: in, out, in, out. Slow and steady. Smooth and perfect. She tried to match her breath to his and, soon, her eyelids started to droop.

"I love you too," she mumbled before drifting off into a deep sleep.

CHAPTER TWENTY-FOUR
Her Own Terms

Ben gently shook Olivia awake. Bags pulled underneath his eyes and lines she'd never noticed before cracked across his forehead. He looked exhausted like he didn't get more than an hour of good sleep.

"Dr. Kim is here. She needs to speak with us," he said.

"What time is it?"

"It's after noon."

What? Olivia groaned and sat up too quickly, blurring her vision. She'd slept for fourteen hours and still had to be woken up. Her body felt heavy and her head felt clouded as if she didn't get any sleep at all.

"It's alright, Olivia. You needed your rest," Dr. Kim said, reading her mind. She moved forward and sat on the edge of her bed. Olivia could tell by her careful movements that she had something important to say.

"Olivia, as you know, we've been monitoring you and Jane all night. This morning Jane's heart rate started to drop. The change is enough to cause me concern. I spoke with Dr. Katz and we feel it's in the best interest of both you and Jane to have an emergency C-Section."

"What?" Bile rose in her throat. Her hand flew to her stomach, hoping to detect movement. When she felt nothing, her pulse quickened.

"I have every reason to believe you and your baby will be fine but I also want to take every precaution possible. It isn't uncommon for a woman with Cystic Fibrosis to have her baby earlier than expected."

Olivia nodded but her mind went blank.

Dr. Kim stood. "I will take good care of both of you, Olivia."

If Olivia wasn't fully awake before, she was definitely awake now. She looked up at Ben. He wore the same anxious face she did. He swallowed often and shifted his weight from side-to-side.

A team of nurses rushed in and surrounded the bed. The flurry of activity was overwhelming and Olivia's heart pounded faster in her chest. She just needed a second, one second to herself to process everything.

"Ben, can I speak to you for a moment?" Dr. Kim beckoned to Ben and led him to a corner of the room.

Olivia craned her head to see what was going on but the nurses kept getting in her way. She tried reading Dr. Kim's lips. *Did she say water or order?* Olivia couldn't make it out. But then Ben looked and her, his eyes bloodshot and dejected. He nodded before turning back to Dr. Kim and she immediately knew: *Are all of your affairs in order?*

Olivia gulped. She thought back to a few weeks before their wedding when they sat quietly, reading over legal documents. Some couples wrote prenuptial agreements. They updated her will.

The bed suddenly surged forward toward the door. She grabbed the side of the bed in a panic. "Wait! Ben! He's coming with me! He's coming with me, right?"

"I'm here." Ben took her hand and followed the bed down the hallway to a set of double doors. "I won't leave your side."

Olivia's heart felt like it was about to explode and she gasped for air. She weakly plopped her head back on her pillow just as a ringing started in her ears. They sped down the hospital corridors but the movements around her were slow and exaggerated. She heard Ben speaking in a hushed voice. He was on his cell phone. She closed her eyes and tried to steady her breathing. *Please let everything be alright... please let Jane be alright.*

Ben pulled his phone away from his ear. "Your father was a grabbing coffee from downstairs but he's on his way. Everything is going to be alright, Olivia."

"Ben?" Her voice cracked. "I don't know what's going to—"

"I won't let anything happen to you."

She grabbed his arm to silence him. "Jane comes first," she said and squeezed with all the energy she had left.

Ben didn't argue. He nodded and lifted the back of her hand to his lips.

The bottom half of Olivia's body was numb but she could feel the sensation of tugging and pulling in her lower abdomen. Bright lights shone above her and a blue sheet hung in front of her face, blocking her view. She felt so vulnerable and defenseless as she lay on her back, drugged and dizzy.

Ben held her hand tight and peaked over the curtain. He was telling her what was going on but she couldn't hear him. She was just concentrating on staying awake. The medication they gave her was doing its job in overdrive.

She watched Ben and smiled sleepily. She wanted to tell him she loved him... to wrap her arms around his neck and kiss him until the room fell away... She wanted to lose herself in his arms...

Suddenly, Ben's face changed. He released her hand and put his hands over his mouth and let them slide to his chin.

What's happening? she thought.

As if he heard her, Ben turned to Olivia. His face was overcome with raw joy. His eyes were bright and his smile looked like it could reach his ears.

A nurse appeared from behind the blue curtain holding a tiny, slimy body wrapped in a thin sheet. Olivia lost her breath at the sight of her. Jane's arms and legs flailed out in every direction as she wiggled around, exploring her newfound freedom. The nurse placed Jane down on Olivia's chest and Ben hovered over them, stoking Jane's head.

Olivia raised her hand to touch Jane's perfect skin but her hand didn't feel like it was a part of her. It was numb and heavy. She touched Jane's face. It was red and scrunched and perfect.

Olivia's vision started to blur and her eyes started to droop, but she fought against it. She didn't want this moment to end.

"Olivia?" Ben touched the side of her face.

A nurse came rushing over and took Jane from Olivia's arms. Another gently pushed Ben back from the table so he could put an oxygen mask over her mouth.

Bring her back to me! Olivia thought but she couldn't form the words. She was too tired. Her eyes were already rolling to the back of her head and she gave into her exhaustion.

Warm air hit Olivia as she entered the neonatal unit and wheeled herself over to Jane. An assortment of machines blinked and beeped, their wires crisscrossing around the incubator. Inside, Jane slept soundly. Her tiny limbs twitched slightly but she was otherwise completely still.

For the past three days, all Olivia had done was eat, sleep, and visit Jane. Friends and family came to visit and Ben rarely left her side. But tonight, she found herself alone and was grateful to have a small window of time to herself.

She locked her wheelchair and reached for Jane through the circular openings lining the side of the incubator. Her skin was buttery soft, practically untouched by the world. Her cheeks were pink and her lips were perfectly full. Dark hair was already beginning to sprout out of the top of her head and her eyes were the color of honey.

Besides her hair and eyes, Jane looked so much like Olivia. It was memorizing. Except, she was so much better.

Olivia was full of joy, fear, excitement, anxiety, hope, and curiosity all at once. But mostly she was relieved. After a few tests, Jane showed no sign of having Cystic Fibrosis. Olivia could now expect her to live a long, healthy, and normal life—a life full of expectations and no limits. She won't have to think before she acts. She can just live.

But Olivia won't be around to see what Jane will become. After the C-Section, she felt as though her body had been broken, just a little bit more. And this break was one she couldn't fix or cover up. Dr. Katz had warned her the months after the birth would be the hardest but Olivia wasn't even sure her body was willing to put up the struggle.

"There you are, Olivia." Her nurse, Calie, had walked into the room.

"Oh, I'm sorry. I lost track of time."

Except, she hadn't. She just wanted to see how long she could stay with Jane until a nurse found her and pulled her away to focus on her own medical routine.

"It's alright. I understand."

"Goodbye, Jane. I love you," Olivia whispered through the openings and slowly removed her hands.

"Would you like me to wheel you back?"

"Please," she said with a sigh.

Calie unlocked Olivia's wheelchair and pushed her forward into a long hallway. There had been something on Olivia's mind and she wanted to take the opportunity while Ben was away to figure it out.

"Is Dr. Katz still around?" she asked as Calie wheeled Olivia into her room. Flowers and balloons lined the windowsill, brightening the dull grey room.

"I'm not sure but I can page him if you'd like. Is everything alright?"

"I'm fine. I just have some questions for him."

With Calie's support, she slowly stood. Her arms and legs shook and her breathing became strained as if she was carrying a heavier load than she was used to. She collapsed onto the mattress. All the energy she gathered to stand melted away and her body was left denser and weaker than before.

By the time Dr. Katz visited her room, Olivia was flicking through television channels absentmindedly.

"Hello, Olivia. You wanted to see me?"

It took her a moment to break her glazed stare and remember exactly why she wanted to speak with him in the first place. "Oh, I..." Her voice trailed off. She struggled to find the right words but ultimately decided there was really no great way to ask. "I want to know exactly how I'll die."

Dr. Katz sunk into a chair across from her. He didn't seem surprised by the question. She supposed he'd gotten it plenty of times before.

"I know it's different for everyone. I just... I want to know what to expect," she added.

Dr. Katz nodded and folded his hands in his lap. "Your lungs will gradually become weaker. You'll notice that it's happening because you'll be exhausted all the time. Simple tasks will take a lot out of you and, though you might accomplish them, you'll suffer for them later."

He looked down at his hands and began twirling his wedding ring around his finger. "Now, if infections don't get the best of you, eventually your lungs will get to a point where they can no longer function. In other words, gas exchange no longer cycles properly. Your lungs won't be able to release the carbon dioxide from your body, which will then build up inside your body and become toxic. This will cause you to become disoriented and confused until you become... unresponsive."

Olivia gulped past the lump in her throat. That was harder to hear than she thought. She looked up at the ceiling as tears welled up in her eyes. You wanted the truth, she reminded herself.

"Thank you for being honest with me," she said.

125

Dr. Katz nodded and stood. His shoes scuffed across the floor as he headed for the door.

"Dr. Katz?"

He turned to look at her while resting his hand on the doorframe.

"Before I become unresponsive and while I'm still aware..." Olivia paused and took a deep breath. "I want to be able to say goodbye."

"You will," he responded without hesitation. You have my word, Olivia. I'll let you know when it's time."

CHAPTER TWENTY-FIVE
Freedom

Olivia held Jane tight in her arms as she rocked back-and-forth next to the bay window in her room. She slept soundly, melting right into Olivia's arms like she was always meant to fit there.

At three-months-old Jane was bigger than ever as if she was never premature. Creases rippled down her chubby little legs and dimples pierced her cheeks. Her eyes were always bright, wide and curious.

There was no such thing as a perfect life, only perfect moments. And this was one of them. Olivia celebrated every second she had with Jane. Whether it was a smile from a funny face she made or Jane's surprise during games of peek-a-boo. Olivia loved watching her wiggle to the sound of music and her fascination with colors and movement.

She looked down at Jane and softly sang. Her cell phone sat next to her on a white changing table and recorded her voice:

> *Wherever you may go*
> *No matter where you are*
> *I never will be far away*

Olivia didn't have much of a singing voice but she wanted to leave Jane a lullaby. She and Ben had made it a habit to record as many moments as possible. It was important to Olivia for Jane to focus on her mother's life, not her death.

"Goodnight, little bug. I love you to the moon and back," she said before stopping the recording.

Using one arm to lift herself and the other to hold Jane, she carefully stood. Just standing and holding Jane drained Olivia of all her energy and her legs shook in protest. She moved the line from her oxygen tank out of the way before gently setting Jane down in her crib.

Olivia sank back into the rocking chair. She felt like she was wasting away and looked like it too. Her cheeks were hollow and her frame was thin and frail. Every move she made was calculated and slow. She had to decide if what she did would be worth the energy.

The sound of a newspaper crumpling made its way from down the hall. Her father understood that she needed time alone with Jane and trusted that she'd call down to him if she needed help. Olivia slept until early afternoon these days so she didn't get a lot of time with her.

Someone had been with Olivia every moment of every day since she came home from the hospital. It made her feel insignificant and incompetent but her lack of strength and constant exhaustion made it impossible for her to take care of a newborn on her own.

Olivia sighed in an attempt to release herself from her frustration. All spontaneity had been taken away from her with the swift decline of her health. Instead, she lived to survive and she survived for Jane.

Olivia pulled a piece of paper and pen onto her lap. For a week now, she'd been trying to write a letter to Jane but couldn't find the right words. She stared at the blank page before her and felt defeated. Shouldn't she have all the answers now that she was coming to the end of her life? But the more she thought about it, the more Olivia realized she had more questions than answers.

Pressing her pen to the paper she wrote: *My dearest baby girl*, then stopped. She tapped the pen against the paper then dropped it again.

That's a good start, she thought.

Olivia looked up and watched Jane's chest rise and fall. Her cheeks squeezed together making her lips pucker. A warm energy rushed through Olivia's veins. She could watch her all night if she could.

Ben's warm hand brushed against Olivia's cheek, waking her from a light sleep. She blinked and watched his face slowly came into focus. His warm chocolate eyes were locked on hers and he smiled.

"Hey there, beautiful." He bent down to kiss her forehead and she leaned into it. "I swear, you can fall asleep anywhere."

Olivia sat up confused. She didn't remember falling asleep. "Hi," she said and rubbed her eyes. "I missed you today."

"I missed you too."

"Is my dad still here?"

"No, I sent him home. It's late. How are you feeling?"

"Exhausted. Help me up?"

Ben lifted her up by the elbows. She immediately got light headed and had to lean on him for support.

"Got it?"

"Yeah, I'm fine," she lied and pressed the heel of her hand to her head. She knew he wasn't convinced but Ben didn't press her.

"How's our little Janie doing?" Ben asked instead, opening up to the crib. He kept one hand around Olivia's waist for support.

"She's amazing."

They both stood over the crib and watched Jane, speechless and amazed.

"I see you've gotten something on paper finally." He nodded in the direction of the letter.

"It's harder than I thought it would be. I can't seem to find the right words."

"They'll come to you. Just give it time," he promised.

I don't have time, she thought but bit her tongue.

"Should I start a bath for you?"

"No, I'm too tired. I'm just going to go to bed."

"Meet you in there?" he asked carefully. He knew she wanted her independence, but also knew she couldn't do most things on her own.

"Yeah, I can do it."

"I love you, Olivia, so much. You know that?"

"I love you too," she said before turning away and slowly walking down the hallway to the bathroom.

Almost immediately, her muscles cramped and she fought for air as her body screamed for her to stop. She pulled her oxygen tank along, using it as a crutch and her hand dragged along the wall for extra support. As her breathing picked up, so did her coughing. She needed to get to Theo before her lungs decided she was no longer worth the effort.

At the threshold of the master bathroom, she erupted into a fit of tacky coughs. The tremor ripped through her lungs and she felt a searing pain in her chest. She covered her hand over her mouth and hoped it did something to stifle the sound. She didn't want Ben to come running.

The coughing fit subsided and she pulled her hand away while taking deep, calming breaths. A flash of dark red interrupted her vision and fear settled deep in the pit of her stomach. Blood splattered across her palm. Her knees become weak but her hands stiffened and balled into fists.

"Damn it," she whispered. Tears fell from her eyes and rolled down her cheeks. She looked into the mirror and saw blood lining her bottom lip. "God, damn it!"

✳ ✳ ✳

Day 26, Olivia thought as she sat hunched over a small table next to her hospital room window. Her father sat across from her as they labored over a 2,000-piece puzzle of a coral reef. It was his way of trying to help her stay focused and aware.

A week after Olivia coughed up blood, pneumonia and a viral infection landed her in the hospital once again and she hadn't been outside for almost a month. A mask covered her mouth and nose, protecting her from impurities but it felt like it was doing a better job of suffocating her.

She desperately wanted to leave. She didn't want her last moments to be in a cold hospital room. But she knew she'd live longer if she stayed.

Any shred of independence she had before she was admitted was gone. Someone had to help her eat, bathe, change clothes, sit up and move in general. She was as helpless as a child and the thought made embarrassment and guilt boil in her stomach.

But she had a plan. It was only a matter of time before Dr. Katz told her there was nothing more he could do. That's when she would stop her medication and say goodbye with whatever dignity she had left. Before she became unresponsive. Before her loved ones would have to hover over her unconscious body and wonder if she could hear them.

Olivia pinched the bridge of her nose as she fought the urge to sleep. It didn't matter that she slept for 14 hours last night. Her body just didn't know how to hang onto energy anymore. Not to mention, she was terrified of falling asleep. She didn't want Ben or her father to walk into her hospital room and find her lifeless body.

She reached across the table for an edge piece. Her boney, grey hand looked foreign to her but she tried to ignore it as she dragged the piece toward another. The two came together with a pleasant snap between her shaking fingers and her arms immediately fell away, exhausted from the task.

"I just remembered that I hate puzzles," her father said as he tried to force two pieces together that didn't fit.

Olivia didn't respond in order to conserve her energy. Instead, she smiled and nodded weakly in agreement. She wanted to spend her final days with friends and family but, at this point, she could barely carry a conversation.

Ben walked into the room holding two cups of coffee. If he was stressed, upset or worried, he didn't show it.

"Hey, beautiful." He smiled and kissed her temple.

Olivia didn't know what beautiful he saw. Her eyes were sunken, her skin was blotchy, and any evidence of muscle had disappeared.

"Amanda is bringing Jane over soon so you can see her," he said and handed a cup to her father.

Jane? Olivia's mind was fuzzy and thick with ambiguity. She could feel her brain tighten under the pressure to remember so she clung to the first thought that came to mind, hoping for release.

"Mom?" she whispered.

But she was confused, both with what Ben was telling her and what she was saying. Her father looked away and shifted uncomfortably in his seat.

"No. Your daughter, Jane," Ben corrected her gently.

The haze in Olivia's mind started to lift and her confusion settled. *My daughter... of course.* She nodded sheepishly.

"Can I get you anything?" Ben asked.

"Freedom," Olivia breathed.

"Okay," he said after a beat. He unlocked Olivia's wheelchair and pushed her toward the door.

Where are we going? Olivia thought but then quickly realized she didn't care. She was just happy to leave the room.

Thrill reflected on her face as they raced down the hallway to the elevators. She hadn't gone so fast in months and it was hard to manage her emotions. A squeal pushed past her lips as she reveled in such a liberating feeling.

Ben pushed her chair through the lobby's automatic doors and outside to a small courtyard. He weaved her chair as fast as he could in loops around potted plants and trees. Nearby, a few hospital employees sat at picnic tables having lunch. They watched, curious and amused.

The warm sun soaked into Olivia's skin. She drank up the Vitamin D gratefully. With all the energy she could gather, she raised her withered arms into the air and closed her eyes. Freedom.

Ben took a sharp turn and she grabbed the armrests with a shriek. She tilted her head back and laughed. It came from deep in the back of her throat and shook her chest. She was breathless. But this time, it felt good.

Ben stopped the chair and moved in front of her. "May I have this dance?" he asked playfully as he held a hand out before her.

She placed her hand in his and smiled. He spun her wheelchair around, moving to an imaginary beat, just like they did on that downtown rooftop a year ago.

It all started with Ben and it will end with him by her side. He made her better. He brought her to life and set her free.

CHAPTER TWENTY-SIX
Goodnight, My Angel

Olivia sat in her hospital bed, propped up by a stack of pillows. Everything around her looked hazy, as if as if she was in a dream. The only thing keeping her present was the heart monitor beeping beside her bed. *Beep, beep.* Like a ticking clock. *Beep, beep.*

Her mouth was covered by a mask connected to a humming BiPAP machine because she could no longer breathe on her own. She had stopped most of her medication and treatments over a week ago and the BiPAP machine had become her lifeline. A continuous stream of air pumped into a mouthpiece that reminded Olivia a lot of what fighter pilots wear. She was fighting, just not in the same way.

Her resting heart rate thumped against her chest at a rapid 130 beats per minute and her CO_2 levels had become toxic, just like Dr. Katz had predicted. Every breath was heavy and painful as if the wind had been knocked from her lungs permanently. She could feel her life slipping through her fingers even though she was hanging on with everything she had left.

Dr. Katz did just as he promised. A few days ago, he let Olivia know that this was the time to say goodbye before she lost all awareness. It was now up to her. She just had to work up the courage to do it.

In the corner of the room, Amanda bounced Jane up and down on her hip. She stuck out her tongue and scrunched her face while Jane just stared at her, open-mouthed.

Burdi walked in front of Olivia carrying a large vase with pink roses over to her bedside table. "I brought you some new flowers," she said as she took away the old ones. Her face was pale and her eyes were bloodshot but her voice was calm and strong.

Olivia turned her head slightly in Burdi's direction and tried to show appreciation with her eyes. Burdi watched Olivia as she rearranged the roses in the vase. Suddenly, she dropped her hands to her sides and slowly sat down next to Olivia. She leaned over and took Olivia's cold, clammy hands.

"It's okay, honey," she whispered, her voice cracking. "You can stop suffering now. You can let go. We'll be okay. I promise."

Relief washed over Olivia. She hadn't known it before, but it was exactly what she needed to hear. Olivia turned her head, even more, to look at Burdi. She nodded as tears filled her eyes. She wasn't ready to die but she was willing to accept that it was time.

Burdi nodded back. "I'll take care of it," she said and stood. "You know, I always wanted a daughter." She smiled and touched her lips to Olivia's forehead, lingering for a moment. "Goodbye, my sweet, sweet girl."

When Burdi pulled away, tears were streaming down her face. She quickly turned and left the room with her cell phone pressed to her ear. And Olivia knew that would be the last time they saw each other.

Amanda rushed over to her. Olivia was ready for her to argue, to tell her she was wrong. Instead, with Jane in one arm, Amanda wrapped her other arm around Olivia and pulled her over onto her side. Then, she gently placed Jane down next to her and backed away slowly without saying a word.

Olivia looked down at Jane, who was blowing bubbles with her tongue. She giggled at the noise, oblivious to the situation unfolding around her. Olivia let herself get lost in Jane's face, hoping to see a glimpse of what she'll look like when she's older. She wondered what kind of woman Jane would become. She wondered if Jane would miss her.

Beep, beep. Olivia's eyes shifted up to her heart monitor. *Beep, beep.*

Pete, Ben, and her father filed into the room. They walked as if they were carrying the weight of the world on their shoulders. She hated seeing all of them like this, knowing that she was the cause of their pain. She looked away and stared blankly at the wall in front of her. At least now she had the power to end it.

Pete walked over and squatted down in front of Olivia. "Hey, champ." He tucked a piece of hair behind her ear and sighed. "I'll never understand it, Olivia. You don't deserve this…" He paused and wiped his nose with the back of his hand. "You'll always be the one I compare every other woman against."

Olivia closed her eyes and begged herself not to cry.

"No clichés," he continued, shaking his head with determination. "No goodbyes. Just a hug and a kiss." He leaned in and kissed her cheek.

When he pulled back, Olivia tapped her mouthpiece. Pete unclipped the device to free it from her face. She took a deep breath and pushed air from her lungs. "Take… care of him," she said just barely above a whisper. "And Amanda…"

"I will. I promise." He pressed his lips to the back of her hand, then stood and walked away.

It was Amanda's turn now. She pulled a chair closer to the bed and sat down. Her face was streaked with tears that showed no sign of slowing down. "I can't do this," she said as more tears boiled over and her head fell to the mattress.

"Yes, you can… " Olivia took a deep breath. "You're strong."

Amanda shook her head.

"Please… for Jane."

Amanda lifted her head and nodded slowly. Her bottom lip trembled as she tried to steady her tears. "I'll take care of her. I promise. No dating until she's thirty and no bikinis."

Olivia smiled and pointed down to her dogwood bracelet, then back up to Amanda. A deep frown pulled at the ends of Amanda's lips but she didn't argue. She reached forward and unclasped the bracelet.

"Thank you for being my best friend… the greatest friend," she said.

"Thanks… for convincing me… to go for it," Olivia breathed.

Amanda smiled weakly. "I didn't—"

"You did," Olivia said. "Now… it's your turn. Don't… waste it. Don't waste… a second of it."

Amanda nodded. "I won't," she said and hugged Olivia before slipping away.

Olivia blinked tears from her eyes as she watched her leave. Amanda immediately fell into Pete's arms, as if her legs had given out. She rested her entire body against his as she cried into his shoulder. He took her waist and led her out of the room.

Olivia's father came forward and took the seat next to her but she didn't want to look at him. She couldn't.

"Even though I knew this day would come, it doesn't make it any easier." His voice shook as tears filled his eyes. "I'll miss you so much, honey." He took her hand and looked down at Jane. "She will too."

"Thank you... for everything. You gave me... so much more than I deserved," she said. "I made it... this far... because of you."

But it wasn't enough. There were so many things Olivia wanted to say to him but it was too hard to speak and too hard to find the right words. She could only hope that they had already been said, that he knew how much she loved and appreciated him.

He leaned in and kissed her cheek. "You've given me the best life, Olivia."

A single tear rolled down her cheek. "I love you, Dad... so much."

"I love you, Olivia."

"To the moon..." Her breath caught and she struggled to bring enough air into her lungs.

"And back," he finished for her.

Olivia looked down at Jane and tried to sear the image of her into her brain. She kissed Jane's forehead, breathing in her powdery scent, and held her soft hands one last time. "I love you... so much little bug," she said.

Olivia could no longer hold back her tears. They streamed down her face as if a dam had been broken.

"Okay," she said and her father took Jane in his arms. He planted one long, gentle kiss on her cheek then turned away.

A painful rip tore through Olivia's heart as she watched them walk away. She could still feel her daughter's warmth in her arms. Emptiness filled her, breaking her in the worst way.

Her heart couldn't take any more. But then there was Ben. Beautiful, perfect, better than any other man she'd ever known, Ben. Just like Burdi, his eyes were bloodshot, but he didn't cry. He took Olivia's face in his hands and kissed her forehead.

How do you say goodbye to the love of your life? She could feel his pain and desperately wanted to take it with her.

"You and Jane are the best parts of my life and always will be," he whispered.

She tried to smile but the signal didn't reach her lips. Her energy was draining fast. "I don't... regret any of it... do you?"

"None of it," he said with fierce conviction.

Olivia closed her eyes as she took a deep breath. "There's so much more... in store for you... I know it. I wish... I could be here... to see it."

Ben looked up at the ceiling then back at her. "I'll see you again. I promise," he whispered.

"I'm so... sorry... for leaving you." Her body started to tremble as her tears gave way again. "I love you... so much..."

He clutched her hand and began crying into her palm. "I love you."

"Kiss me... one last time?"

He didn't hesitate. He took her face in his hands and planted one last, long, slow kiss on her lips. Her heart beat faster and her fingers and toes tingled. For a moment, everything around her was warm and bright. She started to feel strong and whole as if she was coming back to life again. But just as their lips separated, a cold heaviness descended over her once again.

From the corner of her eye, she saw Dr. Katz quietly enter the room.

"Okay," she said, her voice shaking. She turned onto her back but still clung to Ben's hand.

Dr. Katz moved forward and injected morphine into her IV line. Then, he turned off the BiPAP machine and carefully untangled the mask that had fallen around her neck.

"You're an amazing fighter, Olivia," he said and reached to touch her shoulder. He looked down at her and, for a moment, it seemed like he wanted to say more. Instead, he nodded and walked out of the room.

Olivia started to notice how hard her lungs were working. The BiPAP machine sat next to her in an eerie silence. She had gotten used to its hum. Now, the only sound came from her wheezing chest as she struggled for air.

Ben was the only one that remained in the room. She could feel his heartbeat. It pulsed in her ears.

She wasn't sure how long she lay there, motionless and waiting to die. Seconds? Minutes? Hours?

But, eventually, everything started to slow. An overwhelming sense of calm gently washed over her like a sudden rainstorm and lifted the heavy weight from her chest. Her body started to go limp and numb. She wasn't sure if it was the morphine working or her body finally shutting down, but the feeling was a relief. No more struggle and no more pain.

Just like shutting off the lights in a house, room by room, she felt her body shut down one portion at a time. But she wasn't afraid. The calm that had taken over her was powerful and euphoric. Colors and shapes around her looked sharper and more brilliant.

A smile spread across her lips and she turned to look at Ben. "I'll be okay," she whispered to him with what little breath she had left.

He clutched her hand and his breath shook against her palm. She didn't know what would happen next but she knew everything would be okay.

A single tear rolled down her cheek as the shutdown reached her stomach. Her vision blurred but it didn't go dark. Instead, it got brighter like she was staring into the sun. Her breathing slowed but she no longer struggled for air.

There was a sudden tug in her gut that pulled away from her body, like two magnets being forced apart. But the feeling wasn't uncomfortable. It was liberating.

It was truly the most extraordinary moment she'd ever experienced. She remembered no pain. She saw all the good and the bad she'd been given in life and was content.

She took one last look at Ben. She didn't break. She didn't give in. She closed her eyes and embraced death.

My dearest baby girl,

Please know that I love you and miss you so much. I would be lying if I told you that, in the end, I accepted my disease and embraced my fate. I'm angry and devastated that I can't be there with you, to watch you grow and explore this world. And since I can't be there, I wanted to give you a little advice.

First: It's worthless to have love in your head but not in your heart. Knowing what is right and doing what is right are completely different. I hope that you always choose to do what's right.

Second: Love is life's greatest gift. Wherever you find it, don't run from it. Take the risk, hold on to it and never let it go.

Third: Don't compare yourself to others. Everyone has their fair share of successes and failures. Don't let your failures determine your future.

Fourth: Life won't always go as you plan but plan anyway and roll with the punches. Trust me, life goes way too fast even when it feels like it's going too slow. Cherish every moment, the good and the bad. No matter where you end up, it's exactly where you're supposed to be.

Fifth: There's no "right" path, just the path that's right for you. Trust in yourself and always remember that happiness is subjective, love is never perfect, and laughter is always possible.

So there you have it, my own greatest life lessons and I'm passing them on to you. I firmly believe that if you hold these lessons close to your heart you will be happy. I can say this because despite my own missteps, I've loved and I've learned. I can honestly say, without regret or hesitation, that I loved my life.

I'm so grateful to have spent four wonderful months with you. You are a spark of energy and laughter, you are beautiful inside and out, and you have given me more than you will ever know.

Take care of your father. You are his world and he loves you more than life itself, just as I do and always will. You are my greatest achievement and my greatest gift.

I will be with you every day.
I love you to the moon and back.
—Mom

EPILOGUE
The Other Piece

Ben looked down at the old, crumpled photo strip. The four sequential pictures showed Ben and Olivia making ridiculous faces while crammed inside a tiny photo booth during a New Years Eve party. It was right after Olivia proposed to him. Ben had never been so happy in his life and had kept the photo strip tucked away in his wallet ever since.

He traced his thumb over Olivia's laughing face. Love lost is never completely lost. He saw her every day in their beautiful baby girl. He missed her every day. He carried her with him everywhere he went and when he feared he was getting too far away from her, he would pull out this wrinkled photo strip.

"Humans are like puzzle pieces," she told him just before she passed. "They always have more than one perfect fit." It was her way of encouraging him to move on after she passed... to move on from her.

But Ben was lost. He had somehow drifted away from all the other pieces, cramped between dusty laundry machines along with all the vanished socks. And, honestly, he didn't want to be found.

It had been five years and Ben still had good days and bad days. The wound was starting to heal and the pain was only a dull ache now. He didn't cry but he didn't laugh like he used to either.

Part of him wished he could have followed her but that was never his destiny. Jane was his destiny. She was the reason he got up in the morning. She was his life and his purpose. She was the air in his lungs.

Without her, he wouldn't survive.

She tilted her head back and laughed the same as her mom. She even tapped her foot when she was angry or anxious. Her little quirks shook him awake and brought him back to life. They pushed him to be the best father he could be, to guide her and protect her always.

Ben hated that Jane would be cheated of those special moments with her mother. She would only have him to give her sloppy pigtails and drive her to soccer practice. He was the one she would have to turn to for support through breakups and acne.

"Daddy! Daddy!"

Jane's voice cut through Ben's thoughts like a knife. She ran toward him with her arms outstretched, her backpack bobbing up-and-down behind her. She was wearing two different colored socks and her bright blue headband threatened to slide right off her wild head of hair. She took his breath away.

"Hey, baby." Ben squatted down and took her into his arms.

"You'll never guess what happened today," she said breathlessly as she pulled back to look at him.

"What?"

"Well…" she pushed strands of hair away from her face with a flat hand. "Michael kissed me! It was wonderful." She covered her mouth and giggled.

Great. It's started, Ben thought. "Oh, he did, did he? I don't know how I feel about that," he replied.

"He's a nice boy, Daddy." She rolled her eyes and shook her head.

Ben smiled. She shocked him sometimes. Jane was so mature it was like talking to a miniature grown-up.

"How nice? What does he look like? And what's his last name?" Ben feigned police interrogation as he stood and took her hand. Her warmth spread through him like a drug and he was happy again.

"Stop it with the 100 degrees, Daddy." She burst into a fit of laughter, her head tilting back to the sky.

There she was: *Olivia*.

Whenever Jane grilled him with questions he always told her, "Stop it with the third degree." She thought that if she made the number higher it added drama. She'll get it one day.

Her big brown eyes looked up at him and her dark hair shined in the sun. Jane was the greatest gift Olivia could have left him. To her, Ben was perfect and he knew they would be okay.

After all, Jane was his other perfect fit. His other puzzle piece.

141

ACKNOWLEDGMENTS

Special thanks to my good friends Calie, Meghan, and Jordan for reading this book (more than once) before its publication and giving me all of the love and encouragement to finish.

Thank you to my family for being a constant inspiration in my life. All of you are crazy but all of you are my heroes.

Finally, thank you to the brave individuals affected by Cystic Fibrosis who publically share their stories. Your bravery is inspiring and I could not have written this book without you.

Made in the USA
Middletown, DE
12 October 2021

VIEW *from the* EDGE

MEGAN KOZICH